# FELONY

# FELONY

*The Private History of The Aspern Papers*
A Novel

Emma Tennant

Jonathan Cape
London

For Rose & Leo

Published by Jonathan Cape 2002

2 4 6 8 10 9 7 5 3 1

Copyright © Emma Tennant 2002

First published in Great Britain in 2002 by
Jonathan Cape
Random House, 20 Vauxhall Bridge Road, London SW1V 2SA

Random House Australia (Pty) Limited
20 Alfred Street, Milsons Point, Sydney,
New South Wales 2061, Australia

Random House New Zealand Limited
18 Poland Road, Glenfield,
Auckland 10, New Zealand

Random House South Africa (Pty) Limited
Endulini, 5A Jubilee Road, Parktown 2193, South Africa

The Random House Group Limited Reg. No. 954009
www.randomhouse.co.uk

A CIP catalogue record for this book is available from the British Library

ISBN 0–224–06034–1

Papers used by The Random House Group are natural,
recyclable products made from wood grown in sustainable forests;
the manufacturing processes conform to the environmental
regulations of the country of origin

Typeset by Palimpsest Book Production Limited,
Polmont, Stirlingshire
Printed and bound in Great Britain by
Mackays of Chatham PLC

# Dramatis Personae

## CLAIRE CLAIRMONT, 1798–1879

Stepsister of Mary Shelley, Claire Clairmont was the daughter of William Godwin's second wife and became a part of the Shelley household, leaving England when Mary and Shelley did. A love affair with Byron produced a daughter, Allegra, who died at the age of five in a convent in Tuscany. Claire remained a close member of the Shelley ménage up to the time of Shelley's death and the disintegration of the group in the early 1820s.

Claire Clairmont earned her living as a governess in France, Russia and Italy. She lived for many years in Florence with her niece Paula Hanghegyi and Paula's daughter Georgina, whom she adopted.

## EDWARD TRELAWNY, 1792–1881

Traveller, adventurer and author of *Records of Shelley, Byron and the Author*, Trelawny was always on the spot at the most dramatic moments: the burning of Shelley's corpse on the beach at Lerici; and, after fighting in Greece alongside Byron, present at his death in Missolonghi. Trelawny's close association with Claire Clairmont lasted for more than sixty years.

## EDWARD AUGUSTUS SILSBEE, 1826–1900

Massachusetts sea-captain who became an expert on the poetry and life of Shelley. He began visiting Claire Clairmont in Florence in 1872 and became her lodger in order to be in a position to acquire her Shelley papers at her death. The story of Silsbee's experiences and actions in Claire Clairmont's household was relayed to Henry James in Florence in 1887; *The Aspern Papers*, James's novella about a 'publishing scoundrel' and the ruses he employed in order to obtain the spoils of a famous literary love affair, was written in that year.

## CONSTANCE FENIMORE WOOLSON, 1840–1894

Best-selling American novelist of the 1870s and 1880s (*East Angels; Anne; Jupiter Lights; Horace Chase*) and great-niece of James Fenimore Cooper (*Last of the Mohicans*). Known as 'Fenimore' by her close friend Henry James, Constance Woolson spent time with the author in Florence, Switzerland and London. She committed suicide in Venice, aged fifty-four.

## HENRY JAMES, 1843–1916

Born in New York, but lived for more than twenty years in Italy and London, and from 1898 at Lamb House in Rye. One of his shorter novels, *The Aspern Papers* was written in 1887 in Florence and Venice during the time of his close friendship with Constance Fenimore Woolson. It concerns the one-time muse of a famous poet, Miss Bordereau, her niece Tina, and their guardianship of the dead poet's letters and papers in a crumbling palazzo in Venice. A narrator, probably based on Edward Silsbee, gains entry as a lodger and pursues both niece and literary archive, with painful results.

# ACKNOWLEDGMENTS

I am deeply indebted to Lyndall Gordon for her insights and descriptions of the relationship between Henry James and Constance Fenimore Woolson, in *A Private Life of Henry James*, Chatto, 1998.

Other sources include Leon Edel's *Henry James: The Middle Years*, Rupert Hart-Davis, 1963; *Letters From the Palazzo Barbaro*, ed. Rosella Mamoli Zorzi, Pushkin Press, 1998; *Henry James: A Life In Letters*, ed. Philip Horne, Penguin, 2001

For information on Claire Clairmont in Florence:
*Claire Clairmont and the Shelleys* by Robert Gittings & Jo Manton, Oxford University Press, 1992; *Records of Shelley, Byron and the Author* by Edward John Trelawny, New York Review of Books, 2000; *The Clairmont Correspondence*, ed. Marion Kingston Stocking, Johns Hopkins University Press, 1995; *Mary Shelley* by Miranda Seymour, John Murray, 2000; *The Aspern Papers* by Henry James, Penguin English Library, 1984

# AUTHOR'S NOTE

Dates and details in this story of what really went on in Claire Clairmont's household in Florence in the 1870s are as accurate as possible. The sole invention is the visit of Edward Trelawny to Claire in Florence: he had written to her frequently there, stating that he would have persuaded her to banish the fantasy that her child Allegra still lived, 'if I was in your house in Italy', but old age and the rigours of travel prevented him from going. His desire to wring a memoir from Claire which would include her letters from Shelley was strongly expressed by Trelawny when writing to his friend at that time from London.

Georgina Hanghegyi, great-niece of Claire Clairmont, did not therefore meet or become engaged to Trelawny. It is possible to say, given his predilection for new, young brides at regular intervals, that a romance of the kind indicated here could have taken place, the fact of Georgina's relation to Claire and her youth making her a prime choice for the author of the *Recollections*.

The time and places of the writing of *The Aspern Papers* have been changed slightly, with Henry James's visits to the Palazzo Barbaro in Venice given more emphasis than his sojourns elsewhere in the city. Otherwise, he and 'Fenimore' were in Florence and Geneva in 1887 and 1888 as shown.

# Preface
## by
## Georgina Hanghegyi

*My great-aunt Claire Clairmont died only six years ago, but the world to which she had belonged — the world of Shelley and Mary, Byron and Trelawny — had been gone so long by the time I went to live at Via Romana that few people knew Claire was still alive in the 1870s.*

*I was twelve years old when my mother Paula Clairmont brought me from Hungary to live in the house in Florence. Here, thieves, memoir-writers and all those determined to have their piece of the Romantic poets and their circle, jostled for my aunt's attention.*

*In turn, I have chosen to record my own memories of that time through the eyes of the child I was then.*

*Bagnocavallo, Romagna, 1885*

# GEORGINA
## FLORENCE, SUMMER 1876

Aunt has said no one is to go up there today. I am to make no noise. And all of no. 43 Via Romana begins to change, as if a dress has been put on it, and pigtails, so tightly plaited they make the eyes weep, are binding together the shabby old staircase and the rooms where the walls are the colour of dust.

'Showing off,' my mother says, as she stands in the kitchen waving upwards at the floor where Aunt must spend the day gloriously undisturbed. 'Everyone must look at *her*, at eighty-one years old, I ask you!'

I know I don't understand what all the fuss is about, and there's no point in asking. Why is there fresh pasta in the making today, why must I go to the market and buy the cheapest wine, smiling at old Ricardo to get the best possible price? And why am I the one, after being told not to move an inch all day, who must go and let the Americano in? Suppose it's the other Americano, the man with the horrible smell? – 'Do *not* open the door to Captain Silsbee,' my mother snaps at me.

It's still only nine o'clock and the man who is coming to see Aunt is expected at midday. It's a bad time of year for flowers – the heat has killed so many of them off and Aunt sighs, saying it's time for her to go up to the hills, to Fiesole. 'But I can't afford it this year,' she says and she stares first at my mother and then at me. Will the man who comes today bring money? And what – for I've seen it all in the market, the shouting and finger-wagging and bargaining – what will Aunt give the man in return?

The kitchen is dressed up like a bride, when I go in to grab coins for the red wine. Ribbons of pasta are draped over chairs. Bunches of *origani* lie on the table, tied like wedding bouquets with blue satin. What on earth are Aunt and Mama thinking of? Will the herbs turn the Americano drowsy, like Titania and the ass in the story I have read to me upstairs when my great-aunt Claire is in the mood? Will the foreigner who is coming today actually fall in love with an eighty-one-year-old woman? With Aunt, anything is possible.

Still, there are no flowers, and it is this which annoys my mother and will most certainly infuriate Aunt Claire. She can't see the visitor without an array of freesias – or lilies – or the moss roses she says remind her of a garden on the banks of Lake Geneva. I'll be sent to rob the cemetery; it's happened once before – when Captain Silsbee first came to Via Romana. That was because, as I heard Aunt confide to Mama, she considered she'd get a higher rent if the place had plenty of flowers in the rooms.

When it's a day full of secrets like this one, I dream of our farm in Croatia and I think I'd rather be dead than find I couldn't ever go there again. The river Drau, so fierce it can't be gone near in the spring and autumn, picks up speed just at the boundary of our land and plunges down through a deep gorge, with trees so dark they're like my charcoal crayons, standing upright on bare rock. But Aunt found it damp when she bought the farm next to ours, and the whole lot had to be sold. 'My niece Paula Hanghegyi and her daughter Georgina are going to live with me,' I heard Aunt say to Uncle. We're never going to see Hungary – or Carniola – or our own farm again. Why Aunt had to tell her own brother in such a formal way of her plan to 'rescue' us I don't know. It's as if she was trying out the arrangement, or 'adoption', as she likes to put it, for future use.

'It's a good thing if she does adopt you,' Mama half-whispered to me, in the kitchen at home that's so unlike this one: at the farm you could open the door and rush right out into the forest. 'Aunt gets confused, you see. She had a little daughter once, who died. Sometimes she thinks that little girl is you.'

So, in my starched dress with the cuffs and buttons I wait for all the contradictory orders I'll be given today. Captain Silsbee – for he does pay a high rent to Aunt, I heard Julia who comes to clean and cook, exclaim when Mama told her why she must go in and tidy the Captain's room, despite the smell. The Captain, even after the command not to open the door to him, will most certainly be let in. I don't want to think of where he will go next – my mother's room. 'Paula, are you there?' And the reek of garlic and wine and sweat comes at me, even thinking of it. *Don't, Mama, don't* – but the door will close and the Captain will be in there, just waiting to come out and pass me on the stairs with his dreadful wink. At these times I wish I was with my friend, the little dead girl Aunt once had living with her – like I am now.

# Henry
## Venice, Early Summer 1887

High in the Palazzo Barbaro the sounds of the gondoliers are muted, the sun comes in its dazzling whiteness
only just enough to soothe the imagination – for there
are muslin curtains at the tall windows, of the most
exquisite pale pinks and mauves – and the steps of
Mrs Jack's servants as they bring *tisane* or a plain dish
of *risi bisi* to the master, are as exquisitely muffled as
the sounds of traffic on the Grand Canal outside.

An idea – it could perhaps best be described as the
germ of an idea – enters the White Library at the top of
Palazzo Barbaro. It circles, the final flavour to be added
to this monstrous gâteau of a palace, with the soggy
sponge of the basement yielding to increasingly ornate
layers of meringue and ending here, in a wild abandon
of painted ceiling and panels of purest pistachio.

The idea, floating lazily in the filtered whiteness of
the library, sees the recipient of its viral attack at last,
and begins to home in. For, like a giant bundle of
dragées tied together for a christening party, a stout
figure lies under a mosquito net (also pink) halfway
along the polished floor. The siesta hour means the
stomach of the inhabitant of this flirtatious tent rises
and falls evenly, both repelling and inviting the idea
to enter higher up. The sun grows more mellow and

golden, as the afternoon decides to go towards Mrs Jack's dinner hour – and linger for a light *spumante* on the balcony. Zeus, Hera and Leda, all represented on the great ceiling frescoes above the net, look down more dimly in the fading brightness at the God of Modern Literature.

Henry James is grappling with his conscience, when the idea makes its final entry. Didn't poor Fenimore – as the master calls Constance Fenimore Woolson, who has been unrequitedly in love with him for years – didn't the sad (and bestselling) Fenimore declare herself to him in a letter arrived from Florence today? Is her expression of longing the reason for the slight ache, probably indigestion, which ruffles the stomach, permitting the bacillus of the idea to penetrate without being noticed? What shall he do about Fenimore? They can't possibly cohabit – the very word, thought in this library where all the great works of the past serve as a sharp reminder of the unbridgeable gap between a (bestselling) female novelist and himself – causes Henry James to shudder; and, after various efforts to pull himself upright, he succeeds by pulling out a peacock silk pillow and lodging it under his posterior. The mosquito net trembles, its heliotrope glow making a setting sun around the great writer as he stares out to right and left, sensing the presence of an invader.

It had been Lee Hamilton, the gossip in a wheeled bed, who had imparted the story of Claire Clairmont in Florence. 'You mean she lived here quite unknown to us – at least to me,' James had cried, something journalistic in him responding to the sheer laziness of a coterie of writers uninterested in the last, great relic of the Romantic age: Clairmont, stepsister of Mary Shelley, lover of Byron. Down the canal, sounds of surprised laughter can be heard from the Palazzo Mocenigo as this long-dead world comes briefly to life and then shuts down again. (The idea is doing its job: quite without knowing how, Henry James is successfully impregnated.) Agonising over the infatuation and possible consequences of encouraging Constance Fenimore Woolson is now definitely ended, for the length of a novella, at least.

The lips of the pink mosquito net part and the master's legs go heavily and carefully to the floor. Once an idea has come, there must be no question of disturbance, self-inflicted (James has a dread of falling on the highly polished parquet; measuring his length beneath the priceless volumes of Boccacio and Dante) or from outside: even the attentions of young Giovanni, second footman to Mrs Isabella Stewart Gardner, 'Mrs Jack', are now suddenly unwelcome. For the sperm of the idea has reached the great domed egg that is the master's head. There comes a knock at the door. The maid comes in without waiting for a reply.

This is one of those moments Henry James dreads, a moment which reinforces his resolution never to live with a woman, especially Fenimore. For the maid, Tita is her name, succeeds by virtue of her middle-aged bossiness and unappealing appearance in almost killing the bacteria now happily swarming within his bloodstream. With the entrance of Tita, only a nagging worry remains, the original surge of creation banished out into the Grand Canal.

Hadn't the gossipy invalid Hamilton divulged that

the niece of Claire Clairmont still lives – along with the malodorous Shelleyite – yes, James recalls him now, the soapless bore of Florence literary evenings: his name is Edward Silsbee. They don't live together, of course – James shudders again, causing Tita to suggest a *camomili* in case the Signore is catching cold – of course that is out of the question. But he remembers the story. Claire had died, and the Captain, carefully ensconced as a lodger in her house, had hoped for the Shelley/Byron papers at her death. But the price was marriage to the niece. '*Il court encore*,' Lee Hamilton had laughed; and James had chuckled along with him.

The problem, however, remains. If Claire's niece Paula is still alive and the Shelley-spouting Captain too, there is the question of libel to be confronted. The story of the 'publishing scoundrel', a warning to the celebrated and those with something to hide, of the perils of biography – will have to be set somewhere else. And why not Venice? As Tita retires, thwarted in her desire to clean the library, the idea wanders nonchalantly back in through the open window. The evening shouts of the gondoliers can now be heard. The master leaves his shroud of pink netting and walks over to look out.

# GEORGINA
## FLORENCE, SUMMER 1876

'Take it up there and serve it,' Mama says, 'for I won't.' And she goes back into her room and I hear laughter again: for the Capitano as Julia calls him with lowered eyes and a smile I don't like at all, has of course returned from his stroll by the Arno and has gone into my mother's room without even knocking.

Here I am, first told not to move or go upstairs and then instructed to carry the tray right up to Aunt's room – for the visitor has come one whole hour early. He bows to 'Madame Paula' as he names my mother, but she doesn't know later if he is *Americano* or *Inglese* – and she says it doesn't make much difference, they're all after the same thing. 'A light collation,' Mama went on, as if this is really all that people want in the middle of the day – but I see she's changed her mind about telling me what these visitors *do* expect to get from no. 43 Via Romana. In any case, some people come in the evening. 'Our aunt is such an interesting person,' is what Mama says when she sees me wondering at the excitement that's suddenly in our upper part of the old house when they come.

Today, at least, I'm not destined to sit hour after hour in the dreary little room where the smell of ravioli and tomato lingers and the light hardly gets in at all. And I haven't been handed a skipping-rope I've long outgrown and told to go and 'amuse yourself' in the Boboli Gardens outside. I know each terrace and cypress tree – and I hate the fountain with its big, shallow basin, where the Captain from America, Mr Silsbee, starts spouting poems and grows quite wild in the face as he goes on. I'd rather be shut up in the walled garden of the Della Robbias' house out in front of ours, which I can see as I walk up the stairs with the tray – and which is as empty as a nunnery garden, where I sometimes think I would rather be. 'I'm charmed to meet your delightful great-niece, Miss Clairmont,' the visitor says. 'Here, let me take that tray.'

The young man who opened the door was much younger than I'd thought he would be – but then the Captain with the hairs that grow out of his nose like bushes on the edge of a cliff, and his mottled face which goes purple when he says the word Shelley – must be the kind of man I think of when I contemplate men interested in coming to Via Romana. This young man is very good-looking and he has curly black hair, the curls not too tight and his teeth very straight and white. I like him almost at once – and I see him looking at the tray as if he really appreciates the work that's gone into it: Mama's *linguine* with olives and anchovy, the carafe of red wine (the glass needed an hour of soaking before the old dirt would wear off) and the rose, taken by me from the Della Robbias' garden, where I crept in when the watchman wasn't looking. A yellow rose –

'Don't pick a red one,' Mama said, 'or the visitor may get ideas that she's trying to seduce him.' And I heard the Captain give his wheezy laugh from Mama's room off the hall.

'So where did you get this lovely rose?' the young man asks me. And he flushes slightly, as if it might set him off spouting like the Captain. Sure enough – 'What did Shelley write of these beautiful flowers?' he begins – and just as my heart is sinking and I'm preparing to turn and run out of the room and down the stairs, Aunt appears from the alcove near the window and comes over to take my hand. 'Dearest Georgina,' she says, 'you have brought up the tray all on your own!' And she turns to the young man, who now steps forward and says his name is William Graham from the *Nineteenth Century* magazine. They look at me as if I've turned a somersault in the room or flown up the stairs on wings. 'We'll take it over to the alcove,' Aunt says, but still they stand there, while she murmurs 'This is little Georgina' to the visitor. I know this must all mean something, but I'm not sure what.

Aunt Claire is willowy thin and her hair very white like an angel's halo in the sunshine. Her eyes are dark – 'Oh how I wish you weren't all Hungarian freckle and lump,' said Paula unkindly, for she has a good measure of her father's and Claire's looks and I have none. 'Never mind, she'll sell everything she has to educate you, Georgie. You'll just have to learn to look a bit more like her in the face.'

It's while I'm standing there admiring Aunt that I see she actually is flirting with this Mr Graham.

I don't know what the feeling is that comes over me but I don't care for it at all – why, I wonder passionately, does William (for so I already call him in my mind, and dream of walking with him in the Della Robbias' walled garden, safe from prying eyes) – why does William give not one glance to me. 'Sweet girl,' Claire says as she lifts the fork with *linguine*, 'tell Paula we are so much enjoying our collation.' And she laughs merrily, with the sun streaming in on the pasta stained red with Mama's sauce that she makes in one great *pomidoro* squeezing, with basil from the pots on the window sill. She usually forgets to take out the seeds. 'Delicious,' agrees William, and his eyes do alight on me a moment, but it's as if he's trying to tell me to run away downstairs because he has something important to say. I stay there, frozen to the spot, though. I can't help looking at Mr Graham from the *Nineteenth Century*. And he starts to speak anyway, but lowering his voice as if I couldn't hear him if I tried. 'Miss Clairmont, can you talk about your life with Shelley?' William Graham says.

I've only once or twice seen Aunt really angry, and it's a frightening experience when it happens. Paula says she was famous for her rages, once: 'Fiery comet,' Captain Silsbee puts in when she brings the subject up. And Mama makes the cross face she always makes when the Captain quotes with his special voice on. Now I see that Aunt has decided to put her rage somewhere else – the electric storm that was building in her eyes has passed away and she smiles quite cunningly. A glass of the red wine is lifted to her lips. It gleams ruby red in the sunlight.

Mr Graham compliments Aunt on the wine – but of course she's never going to say it's the cheapest Chianti Ricardo could sell me in the market today. I sense that Mr Graham – William – understands he may have gone too far.

'Shelley is in the cupboard,' Aunt says after a long pause.

# HENRY AND CONSTANCE
## FLORENCE – VENICE, 1887

Where the idea had first presented itself was I Brichieri, the house on the hill above Florence that was in reality two apartments – for had not Constance Fenimore Woolson taken the whole house and sublet the lower floors to the Master? – and hadn't the Master given out to correspondents in London as well as to Florentine society that they did not live together at all but were simply neighbours? Fenimore, the celestial neighbour, can be 'called on' but must not be seen, basket of vegetables in hand, as she makes her way up from the humming market to the quiet, pineclad hill. Fenimore did not and never will cohabit with the Master.

But here is the letter, on the floor of the White Library in the Palazzo Barbaro; and here is Henry James, in Venice as the summer performs a crescendo of noise and stink outside. He had hoped to pass the evening deciding whether to go with Mrs Curtis to the Volpi Ball; now he must deal with the idea, as it has settled deep inside him – and he must deal with the letter, too. To calm himself, he will go over to Zattere, where no one he knows could possibly live or stay. He'll follow the winding small canals, as anonymous as the features of people in dreams and as unascertainable as their destinies. They will take him to the end of the story he drafted up at I Brichieri, in a Florence spring Miss Clairmont must have seen – oh, if only he had known it! – so many times before her death seven years ago. But the story has been transposed to Venice now, and the maze of passages and waterways and hidden piazzas will need to show the menace of the hero's intent to rob an old lady and her dim niece of their treasure, the Aspern papers, when the old lady dies. Venice must reach out its slippery tentacles and hold the letters in its grasp; and the hunter, the Silsbee who has formed in James's mind, shall show himself also as one pursued.

This had been the idea; and it is not a pleasant one. James dresses quickly, taking care not to glance up at the magnificence of the Tiepolo ceiling, where nymphs, breasts bursting from their wispy shifts, are chased by Titans, furious and avenging in their lust. One nymph, as James has noted from under the canopy of his mosquito net, has the snub nose and obstinate, devoted expression of Miss Woolson. He will not look. For the truth is, as he knows, and knows all men secretly know – that it is the nymph who chases the god. Poor Silsbee, as the great novelist still thinks of the real-life model for the 'publishing scoundrel' in his coming pages – poor Silsbee will be hunted down by that dreadful niece.

Evening is making purple inroads in the Library by the time James makes his descent into the inner courtyard of Palazzo Barbaro. Last night he dined in Mrs Bronson's gondola, out on the lagoon, which lay like a polished dining-table attended by serenading footmen. This is a world James knows already cannot last. But while Mrs Jack has sway over the Palazzo, and dear Mrs Bronson and her difficult daughter are prepared to sit in their emeralds in the gently rocking boat, he will do his best to join them, despite his need for solitude and disciplined hours. He does love Venice, he must have a room or two to call his own here, one day. But then, Florence – like making love to a talkative woman, he has written from Brichieri to his brother a few weeks back, it is like making love to sit and look out at the Duomo and the spires from his balcony there – Florence has a hold on him which is maybe the stronger of the two. He has failed to add that the amorous mood inspired by this view can only be obtained from Miss Woolson's balcony, upstairs; nor does he record his landlady's reaction to his obvious preferment of the city to herself.

James leaves the courtyard and steps into the Barbaro gondola. He is dressed as inconspicuously as possible, for this wander around the unfashionable side of Venice: the fish market and the tanneries and the houses with shutters closed for so many centuries that they appear as no more than lines on dilapidated faces. The grandeur of the gondola and its recognisable colours will of course give him away, as it sits waiting on the dark slime of green channels choked with garbage and crossed by bridges of crumbling brickwork. People will look down, as they hurry home in the dusk, and see the great, shiny craft which looks as if it has come from the depths of Hades to collect a passenger. But James doesn't mind this: he likes to be incognito and at the same time, known.

As Alberto, the disappointingly short and stocky gondolier employed by Mrs Jack, pulls out into the lagoon, the Palace of the Doges sinking in a satisfying roseate glow behind him, Henry James feels a hardness in his pocket, chafing against his legs. His trousers and coat are tight: he put on weight at Brichieri, eating all the meals Miss Woolson cooked for him. So it is not possible to dig down and remove the offending object, at least without capsizing the boat and tipping both himself and Alberto into deep water. However, he slides a hand into his pocket with difficulty and – watched sardonically by the Venetian who propels the boat towards the Salute, clipping an inferior gondola as he goes – Henry James pulls out a square white envelope from his lower person. Of course! – it is poor Fenimore's letter: he must have absent-mindedly included it in his afternoon preparations. That this has some possible significance does not escape the Master, although it certainly upsets him. But, he decides as he slips it under the red velvet cushion on the adjacent seat – it can serve as a reminder that there is no satisfactory conclusion yet to the idea which has returned to haunt him. What happens in the end to the precious letters and papers, in the story he has taken from Miss Clairmont's Florence and placed here? Does the scoundrel Silsbee get the punishment he so richly deserves? At least, James resolves, as the narrow waterways open up before him and a darkness swallows the smart Palazzo Barbaro gondola, his narrator shall escape the worst punishment of all – marriage to the old lady's niece.

# GEORGINA
## FLORENCE, 1876

Aunt took Shelley out of the tall press she says she
brought with her all the way from Russia. She's shown
me the scratches on the sides that were made when
it was carried down the stairs from her room in Paris.
'But I'll always keep it with me,' she says, and she gives
me a hug as she does when she speaks of this pile of
old papers she calls Shelley. I can understand more
that she'd have a name for the shawl she keeps in the
cupboard as well. It's old and looks as if it might fall
to pieces any minute, but I have a corner of blanket I
hardly use any more now I'm older; and Mama would
laugh at me for holding it when I went to bed at night.
I used to call it my *liebe*. Now, I only take it in when
Captain Silsbee comes. He sits in the armchair in the
room next to my bedroom and Mama's, looking like a
sea monster, all grizzled with drops of water from the
rain outside dripping down his beard. 'Shelley gave
me this shawl,' Aunt told me, the only time she pulled
it out from the dark shelf behind the pile of papers and
the books with red and purple mottled covers. 'It looks
as if it's knitted from moonbeams, don't you think?'

Today I waited for the handsome visitor, the journalist William Graham, to ask why Aunt had promised him he'd see this man the Captain talks of all the

18

time, when there is nothing in the cupboard but old letters and notebooks covered in scribbled writing my teacher would put a great cross against, at the convent school in San Francesca. I know Shelley, the real Shelley, must be in Florence somewhere, because Captain Silsbee is always repeating something he's said. Shelley must be very important, to be quoted in such a loud voice and sometimes for minutes on end. 'That's enough of Shelley for today,' my mother sometimes says, when she can't bear it any longer.

William Graham leant forward and took the pile of papers as if they were almost too precious to handle. It was like mass, when the communion wafer comes right up to my mouth – and I shut my eyes tight, in case I see a miracle. Today I kept my eyes wide open – and I saw at once that William's eyes were closed. 'These are the manuscript books,' Aunt goes on as she pulls a tottering tower of the notebooks from the press and quite recklessly puts them down in front of him. 'Letters, journals, manuscripts of Shelley and Byron.' And I saw Aunt rise to her feet as if to announce that there will be a miracle after all: it will be performed here when she opens the cupboard door and stands in the sunlight like an angel. 'Aunt Claire does love to play the Gürli,' Mama says. 'She thinks the performance will drum up the price of the papers.'

'The words of Shelley are priceless,' Captain Silsbee invariably says at this point – and it's just what Mr Graham says too, when his eyes finally open and he stares down at the mess set in front of him. Aunt has told me a hundred times that no one can beat the beauty of Shelley's writings – though it's hard to see why anyone would want the jumble she hoards here. 'It is of course impossible to put a price on this material,' Aunt goes on grandly.

William Graham pulls out a notepad and a pencil and starts to scribble madly himself, while the papers sit in front of him on the table and give off that fusty smell I caught last night in Mama's bedroom when I went in to say good-night. It's as if something has died in that old press with the Russian carving Aunt is so proud of – it's like when no one could find our canary and it turned up months later in amongst the linen on the half-landing. Today, especially remembering I'd come across the same thing in Mama's bedroom, I felt for nice Mr Graham as he sniffed the air, and then took out a handkerchief and pretended to blow his nose. He didn't like the smell, either. But – and here Aunt pulled out the shawl, giving a light, startled cry as it caught on a nail inside the cupboard door – there is no doubt whatever that the journalist thinks the pile of papers is very interesting, and he's going to write columns about it for his *Nineteenth Century* review. 'Shelley gave me this shawl,' Aunt Claire says, after a quick examination to see if the nail has torn the stitching and ripped the cobwebby pattern, unravelling the whole thing. 'On the night we were at Mr Godwin's – my stepfather's – house and Shelley suggested to Mary – my stepsister as you know – that she take laudanum and commit suicide, while he ended his life with the pistols he then proceeded to produce.'

'No!' says Mr Graham. The shawl kept on lying on the table while Aunt spoke of these terrible things, and

I couldn't help wondering if it had taken the words in, somehow – threats and death plots and all – and was haunted by the dangerous life its owner had had. Poor Aunt! 'I would certainly never sell the shawl,' she says as the sun suddenly goes in and the room darkens. 'My will states that it shall be buried alongside me.'

'So you *do* intend to sell the Shelley/Byron papers?' Mr Graham says, in a voice that is much less dreamy than it had been a minute before. 'Have you settled yet where the collection will go?'

Aunt gave me a piercing look, which meant I should leave the room, and so I did. I'd heard it all before, of course: my education was to be paid for; I was all she had, for she had lost her beautiful little daughter by Lord Byron years before; Allegra had been the name of the child. It was sad, but what Shelley had given her had taken so long to reach her that she had exhausted all other reserves by the time it came – and then, 'I have to confess that the money was badly invested,' Aunt's voice says quite loudly as I hang about on the top landing. Will Aunt suddenly lose her temper and thrust all the papers back in the cupboard, as she did last week when Captain Silsbee went up to see her? I'd only witnessed the very last minute of that scene, as Mama had sent me up with coffee. Or will Mr William Graham be allowed to look at them, pulling the stained old sheets of paper across the table with the sad, grey shawl?

What happens next has me turning and running down the stairs so fast I can hear my own hurtling footsteps behind me, like the sound the big stones make in the riverbed at home, when the torrent comes down and the long, dry summer is over. It crashes in my ears as Aunt shouts and thrusts open the door of her room. 'Paula? Are you there? Come upstairs everybody, come at once! The manuscript book is missing. Thief, thief! Shelley has gone!'

# HENRY
## VENICE, 1887

It's when he's halfway out, across the great lagoon, that Henry James suffers his (now-recurring) bout of panic, that what he sees mirrored in the unmoving depths will come one day and pull him down to lie in shame amongst the dead. Conscience strikes him, here: the domes of the city at this distance are no more than caps worn by clowns and surrounded by the clamour of bells. By writing his tale of privacy molested; of money exchanged for secrets and futures bargained for with wedding rings, has he exposed himself too brutally? Will everyone, in short, recognise the author in the scoundrel who takes advantage of poor and feeble women? – when he had intended, as had seemed so simple to convey, to identify the tale-teller with the famous poet Aspern? Could – more horrible than any of the dreams which now descend from the ceiling of the white library at the Palazzo, to linger in the Master's half-waking brain before lodging in the ancient damask panels on the walls – could readers, friends and worshippers of James, actually compare him to Silsbee, rapist of Miss Clairmont's treasure, destroyer of her niece's happiness?

No, it cannot be possible. Leaving the Palazzo this morning, Alberto had taken his distinguished passenger along the Grand Canal, at the author's own request. He had been asked to pause, while the Signore, fixing his long stare on the façade, had examined Palazzo Mocenigo.

Alberto, like everyone else in Venice, knows that Lord Byron had brought his menagerie there half a century ago, peacocks and all, just as everyone knows that the niece of Byron's mistress, La Guccioli, lives in Venice today. She comes to visit Mrs Bronson, or the Curtises at the Barbaro, from time to time; and Mrs Bronson, who was filling out as Mrs Prest in James's story as they sat motionless on the canal by the striped pole of Mocenigo – Mrs Prest like Mrs Bronson must be chatty, compelled to inform the eager bounty-seeker of a way to obtain the letters and papers of the fictional poet who will replace Byron and Shelley. 'Go and take rooms with the old lady,' Mrs Bronson/Prest says in James's ear; and he smiles until he remembers this is not invented: it's just what Vernon Lee's brother had told him actually happened, when Captain Edward Silsbee came to Florence and moved in with Miss Clairmont. James groans aloud: how can he not be mistaken for the bounder? 'I heard last night that the niece of La Guccioli has just burnt a letter written to her aunt by Byron, due to its improper content,' Mrs Bronson's words from last night come back to him. It's too bad: on the one hand, everything that sheds light on private desires and shared memories should be destroyed, so James thinks; and he's tempted to discuss the matter with Alberto, who has taken him right out into the lagoon without asking where the guest of Signora Curtis would like to go. On the other hand it is surely vandalism to burn the thoughts and declarations of a great man? 'Where are we going?' Henry James cries, as his panic grows by the minute and the lagoon grows along with it, to stretch out wider than the sky. 'No, I don't want to go to Torcello.'

By the time the gondola has edged its way to Rio Marin – 'Here, here,' James instructs his now-yawning pole-bearer, in waters as constricted and claustrophobic as the lagoon had been immensely vast – 'here!' And he points in triumph at a palace so worn down and faded in appearance that it seems to him to resemble the inmate he shall place there: a dancer at a long-forgotten ball; a hoarder of the brief passion of a poet long dead, but inspiring love still, as she cannot. 'This is the home of my Juliana,' James informs Alberto; and he sits back, content at last, as the soft sussurations of stagnant black water lull his return to the Grand Canal, at least forty minutes away from this unfashionable district. 'And a *garden*,' Alberto's Signore Americano breathes ecstatically. For doesn't he have Mrs Prest remark that one in search of the spoils of these unwitting victims should have some good excuse for forcing himself – not to put too fine an expression on it – into the seclusion of their home? 'Say you intend to rescue their garden,' Mrs Bronson had gone on with her accustomed briskness. Now, as Mrs Prest, she received the news that in Rio Marin such a house did exist – and a small garden did indeed lie alongside it. 'The tale will go well,' the fictional Mrs Prest says pointlessly to her author as the black boat skims along.

Nevertheless, the possibility of scandal – even of obloquy – has not been removed. Today, as he stood by the green damask panels of the white library and saw himself in the long, splendid mirror, James had not doubted himself to be model and inspiration for Jeffrey Aspern, the American poet whose letters form the basis of his plot. In Aspern the first, glorious freedom of his native country had come to be expressed; none but James, achieving with prose the heights arrived at in poetry by his predecessor, could be spoken of in the same breath as Aspern. It had been daring, to place an American as the famous poet and long-extinct lover of his Juliana, the relic who lives on in the faded emptiness of Rio Marin. But, with Henry James as an example of what can be shown to excel – even if exiled to distant Italy – America could stand proud in the eyes of the world. Henry James *is* Jeffrey Aspern – a fresh, unforgettable new voice resonating from a still young and backward country.

So how – this the Master asks himself as Alberto helps him from the gondola and he walks stiffly up the lovely, curved staircase, eyes watering slightly at the promise of *gnocchi* and, one of his favourite dishes, *fegato Veneziano*, liver cut small and fried in Italian oil with the sweetest of small onions – how could the creator of one as distinguished as Aspern possibly be confused with a Shelley-spouting pirate by the name of Silsbee?

'Shelley, that's the answer,' James announces to a surprised footman, who leads him gliding to the *sala* where Mr and Mrs Curtis will welcome their illustrious guest to luncheon. 'I need to ensure that Aspern has more Shelley in him than Byron.' For passion is one thing – and Juliana must indeed have experienced it with her great American poet. But too much of it –

crass, over-reaching, acquisitive passion – can lead to a character not unlike that of the dread sea-captain, Edward Silsbee. A distinguished author bears no relation to one who seeks his fortune in long-buried scandals. 'And no doubt Miss Clairmont had a love as great for Shelley as she did for the other,' James reassures himself as he bows over Mrs Curtis's hand, seats himself by the long window looking out on the happy traffic of the Grand Canal, and gazes at Tita as she enters with the *gnocchi*, a footman following with silver bowls of *radicchio* and cheese. Hadn't there been some story of a child born to Claire in Naples – a child said to be fathered by Shelley? Doubtless she had hoarded that secret along with her other papers, those everyone knew about that dealt with little Allegra, her child with Lord Byron. This sort of thing will on no account be included in *The Aspern Papers*, of course.

But for a moment, as he begins to give a long – and possibly exhausting – account of this morning's outing in the Barbaro gondola, Henry James finds himself wishing it was all true, and not a story after all. If it had been he, and not Silsbee, who had ingratiated himself into the little household at Via Romana – and it had been he who observed, like one visiting an ancient burial site at the moment of disinterment, the features and gold raiment of a legendary warrior, would it not have been grand?

And for a while the author falls silent, and even goes so far as to restrict his second helping of *fegato* to a forkful. What, after all, if he had really been there; and could simply have told the truth?

# GEORGINA
## FLORENCE, 1876

Mr Graham has gone. He looked very white when he came down and stood by the kitchen door and a loop of pasta my mother must have forgotten about brushed the top of his head. She'd hung it from the ceiling – I remember now, that was when the Capitano came in and he laughed to see her standing on a chair. 'Paula, you've better legs than I'd imagined,' he said and I ran away to my room, though I can hear them from there too. There's something Captain Silsbee wants and my mother won't give him, like everything at home these days, with Mr Graham wanting Shelley and the Captain wanting Mama if she'll give Shelley to him.

Otherwise, the *linguine* is all eaten and there's a smell of tomato sauce, the Napolitano the Captain likes to boast he knows the name of. For since he came here there's been a ban on Bolognese which used to be my favourite. No, tomatoes and basil – and 'Georgina, go down to the courtyard and find the oregano' – this is all I hear when Mr Silsbee comes. And he comes every day. 'We may take a trip to Naples,' he says to Mama, and he gives her a great pinch on the bottom, which I hate to see. 'You can come too, Georgina,' he adds; but I run to my room

28

again, for the Captain likes to pinch as much as to wink. None of us is safe here, from this horrible man. 'Napolitano,' I hear him say yet again as he makes his usual entrance, brushing Mr Graham from the entrance to the kitchen. 'How was it, young man?'

William – as I shall call him, for I see he is shocked by Aunt's recent tantrum and is in need of a friend – still looks very pale but it seems he can't move from the doorway, with the ribbons of white pasta making a kind of crown that slips down over his eyes. 'You recognise, of course, the significance of Percy Shelley's "Neapolitan charge",' Silsbee goes on, and by the lilt his voice takes on, I know we're in for a recital. But this time, luckily, I'm wrong. 'We need to go to Naples,' Silsbee says, going down to a whisper and walking over to William, even going so far as to grab his sleeve. 'We need to know the paternity of the child Elena Adelaide, registered in Naples as the daughter of Percy and Mary,' he says as if this could be really urgent. 'But she was no such thing, naturally.'

William shakes his head and gazes across at me. Then, with all of us standing and staring, he opens his coat and we see a plain waistcoat and a watch chain draped across it. He starts to flap the pockets of his coat, to show there's nothing in there. 'Please inform Miss Clairmont that I have not removed the Shelley manuscript book from her keeping,' he says in strangled tones, as I find I can't help wondering why Mr Graham of the *Nineteenth Century* should have elected to wear an overcoat on such a hot day.

'You may search me if you require further confirmation,' poor William goes on, still talking as if someone's thumb and finger have a hold on his windpipe. But I'm beginning to suspect that Mr Graham would have liked to fill the deep pockets inside his coat. 'I'm sure that will be quite unnecessary,' Captain Silsbee says, sounding like the proprietor of the house – of Aunt – and, of course, of Shelley. I see even Mama is annoyed by the way the Captain talks. Then, just as I realise with a dreadful sinking feeling that there's a perfectly good reason for the Captain to be convinced of the innocence of poor Mr Graham, there are steps on the stairs. Both Mr Graham and the Captain look frightened, and their eyes keep swivelling round the kitchen, as if they're looking for a way to escape. 'The Fiery Comet herself,' Silsbee says, but too low to be overheard. He tries to put on a satisfied laugh.

'Ah, Mr Graham,' Aunt says as she sweeps in – there's no other word for it. She looks fresh and pretty, and I can smell her cologne. I could also have told the Captain and Mr Graham both, that Aunt's rages don't last long. 'I am pleased to see your Aunt like this,' the Captain says in a low voice to my mother. 'This, one hopes, was the last of her great fits of anger. They cannot be good for her, at her age.'

But Aunt has taken Mr Graham into the dark little dining-room next door as if nothing at all has happened. She glances once, coolly, at the Captain as she goes. I know she has understood he wants her dead – so that when she dies, he's in place to get the rest of Shelley. And I, I am the one who knows the Captain sent Mama up, all of three days ago, to Aunt's room in the hot hour of afternoon sleep. He told her she was to open the cupboard Aunt has said no one must ever open but herself.

The voices go on, low and serious, in the dining-room where Julia comes round with food heated up – always heated up – for I know by now that Aunt has completely run out of money. The smell of the food lies in the room, and at one point I hear someone rise to go over and pull open the shutters and then the long window that looks out on the garden. I know it is Mr Graham, because he opens the door as well, to admit a draught of air – and as he turns to go back to the table to sit with Aunt he says, 'You mention this as the Della Robbia garden?' and I imagine he points at the walls and well-arranged trees and flowerbeds where I sometimes think I see Allegra, poor Aunt's dead daughter, as she walks round and round. A murmur comes: Aunt must be agreeing that it is indeed the garden of the Della Robbia house; and then, after a pause for thought, Mr Graham says, 'There is surely a connection with Shelley here? Didn't Emilia Viviani belong to the Della Robbia family – did she not come from here?'

And as Aunt says, with weariness in her voice, that yes, Emilia Viviani did come from that house, the door closes and the voices fall to no more than a hum again.

They're the same, William Graham and the Captain: they want anything they can lay their hands on from Aunt and then they wish her to die.

I stay alone in the kitchen, I cannot even go into my room. For next door are the Captain and Mama, doing what they did after she brought him the Shelley book down the stairs in the afternoon sleep time. Once this hot weather has set in, you can hear everything in 43 Via Romana, the awnings are up but the windows are open. And Mama's knees poked up either side of Captain Silsbee; pink and shiny as the bald patch on the back of his head, when I looked in. The manuscript book lay by the bed on the mother-of-pearl inlaid table Aunt brought from Russia when she came to live in Florence. And I screamed – but Mama was screaming louder and she couldn't hear.

# CONSTANCE
## I BRICHIERI, FLORENCE, 1887

Constance Fenimore Woolson is herself a niece of a famous writer, James Fenimore Cooper; and she knows by now, since hearing the murmurings of the Master in the study of the house he pretends he does not share with her, that nieces are somehow involved in the novella he has drafted through April and May. Deaf to the nightingale in the wooded slopes below, which Miss Woolson discreetly – and frequently – pointed out to her great friend and mentor; blind to the fireflies that danced about on the terrace at the house which he so frequently visits but never mentions in his correspondence to London friends or to family, James has been exclusively occupied with constructing the necessary personality of a niece. Miss Woolson is also dimly aware that the chief protagonist of the tale is based on a man she has met several times in Florence; that this man, Captain Silsbee, had paid an exorbitant rent to poor Miss Clairmont in return for a possible plundering of the Shelley and Byron letters at her death; and that he had run at spectacular speed when informed of the price of the archive, following Miss Clairmont's demise. Paula, the dark, angry-looking woman Miss Woolson recalled having seen once or twice in the Uffizi with her daughter, a lumpy, red-haired girl, was the name of Miss Clairmont's niece. This niece had proposed marriage, as the sole way Captain Silsbee could lay his hands on the spoils. All Florence had laughed at the speed with which the devoted Shelleyite had run, never to be seen again.

Now Miss Woolson, or 'Fenimore' as Henry James refers to her, feels herself to be a niece in a similar situation. It is early June; HJ – as she in turn thinks of him – has been gone one whole week longer than the ten days he promised, before leaving for Venice to check (perhaps) on some details of his story, which is set in that city. HJ of course, did not really promise; that would be most unlike him; but there was a look, so Fenimore thinks as she sits alone on her terrace, in the eye of the great man as he left, which betokened both terror and forthcoming confirmation of love. Once the remote palazzo, occupied in James's tale *The Aspern Papers* (as Fenimore knows it will be called) by two spinsters so far removed from physical passion that the garden, once alluded to in excitement by Henry as he sat with his hostess in the twilight at the Brichieri, becomes the surviving symbol of growth and bloom – once these ladies, each as old as the other, as Fenimore instinctively feels them to be, are checked on by the magnificent author, it will be time for his return. In the strong – but immediately censored – imagination of Constance Fenimore Woolson, there will be a closer coming together of Henry James and herself. There may – but she doesn't go as far as this, it is in fact totally unimaginable – be marriage. In either case, there is no need to continue forever as a niece.

The difficulty in considering this possibility is increased

by the prolonged absence of Henry James. Fenimore walks the length of the terrace, looking out on three sides at the vista with which – or whom – the Master so delightedly communes. Someone – Lorenzo, perhaps, for it's tiresome to have no one but a spinster to cook for: spinsters ask for salads and flinch from the *dolce* and ice creams Lorenzo loves to perfect in the kitchens of the Brichieri, folding a sugar-candy swan into a lake of palest custard – someone has placed a bright blue morning glory in a pot near the French window where Henry and Fenimore are accustomed to emerge from the building to take the air. So vulgar! Fenimore can hear her friend's murmur of disquiet, at the trumpets as blue as the Quattrocento sky at noon. Only the badly bred have morning glory staked along their mean balconies and tiny gardens. Fenimore bends to remove it from its – equally humble – terracotta pot.

Even as she does so, her brother's voice rings in her ear: has the brazen climber inspired a memory of his insistence that she promote herself more, and learn not to shun publicity, as she has been wont to do? 'Give the interview to *Harper's* that they asked for,' the voice says. 'And a photograph. Come on, Connie, you should do this. Think of your sales, after all.'

Miss Woolson bridles as she holds the slender stalk of the bright plant a minute, before deciding whether to condemn it to life or death. The blueness, the total lack of subtlety of the flower, does seem now to represent life – though she can be certain Henry James will not have placed it in the garden of the old ladies who guard the poetic passions of the past. Even the crudest treasure-seeker (as she senses James

35

does not wish his protagonist to be) would balk at instilling a morning glory under the nose of his ethereal victims, aunt and niece. 'I don't know,' Fenimore mutters feebly, as she remains in her bending position and is caught there by Lorenzo, who emerges on the terrace with a face of thunderous boredom. The Signorina's omelette is ready, in the dark and shuttered dining-room downstairs.

'Thank you, Lorenzo.' Miss Woolson straightens and attempts to recover poise. This is now not the time to ask if a message has come from the Signore – and she knows this is not how she should refer to HJ, for it makes him a husband and just what Lorenzo would like.

All through the careful luncheon, with its bottle of *aqua minerale* and single peach, Miss Woolson ponders the two questions: whether she – as a best-selling author, after all – should lose her perfect reticence and taste, and let her public in on her private life. She shudders at the thought. Or – when dear Henry returns – should she declare herself to him, more even than she has done in the letter recently sent to Palazzo Barbaro? But this prospect is as unlovely as the morning glory: as brazen and as lacking in charm. It is impossible to decide, either way: a professional author, thus losing femininity and reserve, or prospective wife? Or will she go on as before – and end a niece?

As Fenimore – fatally – picks up her pen in the little study next to the dining-room where her peach lies half-eaten on a plate on the sideboard, the future recipient of her next and disastrous letter sits snugly at the Lido conversing with the Countess Pisani. How far from poor Fenimore is this beautiful woman, daughter of a French odalisque from the harem of the Grand Turk – and there is a link with Byron too: the Countess's father bled the poet to death at Missolonghi – how immeasurably distant from the clever but submissive Miss Woolson! They could be two different sexes, James thinks as he returns the Countess's bold gaze and checks at the same time that the Curtises' gondola still waits for him: Alberto had made a muddle the other day of instructions to linger in the Canareggio while the Master breathed in the atmosphere, and there had been an embarrassing haggle with the gondolier finally hired in an insalubrious backwater; all this had been highly distracting to one drafting and polishing a tale he knows to be superb. 'I so agree,' the celebrated author murmurs to the Countess – although he has no idea of what she has been speaking. She had been married to a much older husband; she must be used to absent-mindedness. But she is delightful, after all: a romantic

37

heroine from the English novels James is determined not to emulate. How – how irretrievably *American* dear Fenimore seems, when one has passed a few hours in the company of Countess Pisani! And to think he had contemplated marriage – no, he corrects himself and allows his mind to hover between nieces, Miss Tina in the novella to which he is now devoted day and night; and the stocky, snub-nosed niece of J. F. Cooper – no, he had never promised or suggested marriage to Miss Woolson. Then his mind skips again and settles on a further cause for shame. Is not Jeffrey Aspern the name he has selected for the great, long-dead poet whose letters the Misses Bordereau conceal and use as bargaining chips, raising his hapless protagonist's rent as they go – is not Jeffrey simply J. F. lengthened but not disguised? Will poor Fenimore recognise herself in Miss Tina, after all?

'What is it, Mr James?' The Countess is smirking and fluttering a printed menu card, a houri who suddenly gets on James's nerves. He rises; bows over her too-white hand. Fenimore is a worker; when she's not writing her (alas! not really of the first order) novels, she's gardening, planting and digging like the pioneer she is. Wherever Fenimore goes, she puts down roots, then moves on, Henry muses. The Countess is as decorative and useless as a butterfly. And of course the doughty Miss Woolson will not mistake herself for Miss Tina, niece of the ancient lover of Jeffrey Aspern, his 'Juliana'. She is no relation of the invented hero of American letters – how far-fetched, he concludes in disgust at himself as a disappointed Countess turns her head towards him, an exotic bloom reaching towards the sun. 'You will dine with us on Thursday' come the words faintly whispered by the woman he will later describe as 'widowed, palaced, villaed, pictured, jewelled and modified by Venetian society'; and he pauses a moment (Yes! There is Alberto, snoozing in the grand gondola in the sun; James lifts a finger, pulls his white handkerchief from his breast pocket and gives a discreet wave) before announcing with extreme regret that he is contemplating leaving Venice on that day. Padua perhaps? – he thinks of Shelley – and, if they had been lovers, the poet and Claire Clairmont, then the Villa d'Este in Padua would have been the place where they had made love. 'I go to the Villa Malcontenta,' James says instead to his Countess.

The trouble is – and this Henry James feels must somehow be connected with the distinctly dangerous new topic he has chosen for his fast-growing, scandalous tale – the trouble lies in the new vulgarity and brazenness to be found even at the highest levels of society these days. He had been shocked by May Marcy McLellan, daughter of the Civil War general after all, who had written a long and gossipy 'letter' for a New York newspaper, containing all the half-secrets of the world she had visited; yet the Countess still invites her, and so do the Morosonis, described as selling their villa to a hotel owner for 'pecuniary reasons'. Did people no longer care that their finances and love lives were spilled out in the columns of a New York rag?

And in what way am I different from this smart, forward girl? James asks himself as Alberto's pole sinks expertly in the pale blue waters of the lagoon. Tiny fish dart along the ridged sand of the seabed just a few feet below. Am I not as transparent as the worst, over-encouraged, thinking-she-can-write-and-that-her-writing-has-any-business-to-exist American girl? Won't poor Fenimore see, as soon as she opens the pages, her own desperately unsophisticated and unalluring person, clumsily disguised as Miss Bordereau's niece? And – worse still – won't all her acquaintance see it too?

'*Basta*,' says Henry James loudly, as the gondola glides past the Doges' Palace. He remembers briefly that the Countess's late husband had been descended from the Doges, and is calmed by the reflection that history is all around him – far from gossiping girls or spinsters who may take offence at what he writes. History – and its companion, literature, are more important, after all.

So, as Miss Woolson, in the magnificent but lonely sunset at I Brichieri, hands Lorenzo the offensive morning glory (now drooping in the beginning of its nocturnal death throes: as Fenimore terms it; the trumpets sound their azure note all day and then die when the sun goes down) her anticipated visitor makes his final decision not to return to Florence to enjoy her company. He'll simply take off: it will do him good to get out of Venice.

'I shall make a little *viaggio*,' James announces to his hosts at dinner – when a Venetian sunset, reminding him uncomfortably of the deserted Miss Woolson on her empty terrace in Florence, has been witnessed and the meal is under way. Something in the great writer makes him want to see the house where Claire and Shelley met and – perhaps – made love. Not

that anything of this will be transmuted into Miss
Bordereau and Jeffrey Aspern – Miss Tina/Fenimore
might get ideas, of passions still undeclared and burning
in Henry James.

# GEORGINA
## FLORENCE, 1876

I have decided to run away, and I shall take Allegra
with me. She waits at the top of the stairs and I
know from the news she gives me that we shall
go to Venice and then to a villa in the hills not
far away, where there will be sunlight and air and
nothing will be like the life here, in the grey walls
of Florence.

It was when I was sent up to steal Aunt's letters
and papers that I first saw my little friend, who
cannot be more than four years old, but has a
gravity that belongs to another age, along with her
pretty dress and the lovely frocks her doll wears
when she holds her out for me to inspect. We are
taught nowadays to respect our elders and superiors
– at least most children are, but Mama, of course,
lacks any knowledge of how to rear the young, and
Aunt has herself returned to childhood: gay some
minutes, imperious the next. Allegra's demeanour is
taught her by the Sisters at the convent, so she says,
and it is exemplary, though I could never copy it.

Her eyes are so blue Aunt says they were compared
by Shelley to an Italian sky. And it is this blue gaze
I first saw when she came onto the landing to meet
me. I carried a letter from Lord Byron to Aunt in

my hand. She caught me as I tried to slip this cruel letter in my pinafore. Byron informs a man named Hoppner that he will place his daughter in a convent, he talks of money and dowries and I could not feel this man who lives with a wolf in his palazzo in the watery city, could have loved his little daughter at all. But she looked up at me, very pale, and said she had liked the Contessa Teresa and she had enjoyed the Carnival on the day it snowed – but most of all she loved Este, the house with the garden we will run to, while Aunt dozes after her latest interview with another journalist as impressed as the foolish Mr Graham, and Mama and Captain Silsbee are together in the room next to mine, the room I hope never to have to see again. There are ripe figs, in the garden of this house I Cappucini, where Allegra will live again, with her mother when she was young and full of hope and fear. Grapes hang right down by the summerhouse, where Shelley writes his rhymes, just for Byron's daughter. And if Aunt could know her one and only child stands now waiting for me – then she might wake like Sleeping Beauty, and find herself as young as she had been when all those letters and poems were quite new.

Aunt thinks she still lives then, sometimes, and I wonder if she sees me when Mama and Captain Silsbee send me up, to plunder the box in the old Russian press. She's in a trance, I decide, as I pull out the faded letters from Shelley ('I only want Shelley, don't bring me down the correspondence of that wretched consul in Venice and his wife. The Hoppners bore me to distraction,' Silsbee roars at me if I come down with the wrong spoils). I get the feeling that Aunt's dream has taken her back to that villa at Este, where she and my new friend Allegra were happy; and even, on occasion, to the shores of Lake Geneva, when the big storm raised ideas from the heads of all in that haunted house by the lake. 'That was where the monster came, bolted together by lightning flashes,' Aunt said to me once, when she caught me creeping out of her room, a pencil-written notebook in my hand. (But Silsbee didn't like it, and it had to be returned: 'Whatever do I want with the wretched Mrs Shelley's scribbles?' he yelled, and I could hear Mama laugh.) 'Shelley it was who put the Latin words his wife could not have known, into the childish tale,' Silsbee shouted on, as I ran back up the stairs to restore the notebook where it belonged. Why did I always think, on these occasions, that Aunt's eyelids had been slightly open at the time of my theft: that she saw me, but was lost in that past of nearly sixty years ago, before Allegra's blue eyes were briefly, brightly, in the world? Surely, poor Aunt had entered another time – otherwise she would have restrained me as I tiptoed out with the trophies Mama made me steal, under pain of sending me to live with my other aunt, dull Ruth, back in Hungary.

When this semi-conscious state takes hold of Aunt Claire, her room at the top of the house seems to change its shape and it becomes the villa or palazzo the letters speak of: the Mocenigo, in Venice, where the man she pleads with so painfully, in the box in the chipped old cupboard, lives and sneers at her pathetic cries to be reunited with Allegra. Or there's a house at Lerici right by the sea – but it's cold and unfriendly there, and it's where Aunt receives the news of her daughter's death at the convent in the marshes of Romagna, Bagnocavallo. I see the terrace and hear the lapping waves on the shingle and sand. Then I see bodies on the beach, and a bonfire. The pupils of Aunt's eyes move, under lids the colour of tobacco leaf, so old and thinly stretched have they become.

It's in these moments that Allegra comes to me. If Aunt is awake, and going through her routine – so unlike Mama, she is always reading, and makes notes for me to follow: Read *Rasselas*; take G to Library for translations,' in her desire to provide me with an education – then the child Allegra will on no account appear in the room. Maybe, like me, she simply hates the visitors and callers who force their way in here, all after Aunt's treasure, her box of words by the great poets, both so long dead.

Today, Allegra is at the top of the stairs as I go up. The Captain, calling out from Mama's room next to the kitchen, demands I go in search of a letter Shelley wrote from Naples, describing his visit to Mount Etna. 'Your blessed aunt was carried up the mountain on a litter,' Silsbee calls after me, and he says, 'Paula, Miss Clairmont is a charming woman, but I assure you she conceals the birth of a second bastard daughter, little Elena Adelaide, at Naples. How else would a strong young creature such as Claire be in need of a litter to take her up there?' And for once, I hear a hesitation before Mama quickly agrees with everything the Captain

45

says. Will she marry him one day? But I will be far away – with Allegra in the house where once there was happiness, and an abundance of grapes and figs.

'Oh I don't know,' Mama says feebly. 'Who was the father then, Edward? Not Lord Byron again, surely?'

Silsbee laughs. He's a huge man and I can hear the bed shake as I make my way past the first-floor landing. 'No, Shelley was the father, you fool,' Silsbee trumpets, so I imagine Aunt will be woken from her journey into the past. 'There's plenty of evidence – we need more.'

'But how?' Mama asks plaintively. I reach the last flight of steps and gaze upward. Allegra is standing there waiting for me. She wears a woollen jacket over her dress, ready for travelling.

'Shelley and Claire were alone together at the villa in Este three weeks,' Silsbee replies – 'when Shelley lied to Byron and informed him he and Claire had come to visit little Allegra, bringing Mary Shelley and her two children with them. But they came alone.'

The child descends and places her hand in mine. We go quietly down, past the kitchen and the cramped dining-room with the smell of *pomidoro* from the Captain's unending Neapolitan pasta.

And I think of the stain of red sauce at the corners of his mouth when he eats, and of the blood that runs down the legs of the young woman on a litter, carried up over black pebbles and lava dust to the fire that belches out of the top of the volcano, on Mount Etna.

Then I open the front door and we creep out. Aunt has not woken. Mama and the Captain have gone into the kitchen and a pan goes on, to boil water.

# HENRY
## ESTE, SUMMER, 1887

This is a last journey before the unreal but unfortunately necessary Jeffrey Aspern takes over the story of poor Miss Clairmont's papers. One last time, before covering one's tracks entirely, to do the concupiscent research the Master has stated he disapproves of so strongly: the hunting down of lovers' dates and trysting-places; even the scent of a pregnancy. And – for James at least – the most important haunting of all will reveal itself at the Villa I Cappucini: the ghost not of the image (photographs, with their deathly reminders of the pointlessness of life and the fixed date of its ending presaged by the clicking of a shutter, fill him with boredom and dread) but of the pen, where it was moved to write such masterpieces as *Julian and Maddolo* and *Prometheus Unbound*. Here, Shelley left Claire's side and crossed the sunken lane to the ruins of the Gothic castle where once the Medicis had lived, and then returned to the privacy of the villa's summerhouse to write. Alone; undisturbed. No, it is hardly possible to make a Jeffrey Aspern of the slender, beautiful poet, especially here, where perhaps he and the Fiery Comet had made love. And how can the 'Juliana' into whom the vigorous, shining-eyed Claire Clairmont must be transformed, be shown convincingly to be American?

His tale rears up and lies flat again, a fold of paper masquerading as the real thing. As for Miss Tina, she is the sole character he can believe to come from his native land. Because she is, and he shudders, standing at the gate of I Cappucini (a carriage waits on the dusty road, the driver lolling half-asleep on his seat), she is of course based on his dear friend, Fenimore.

The thought of Miss Woolson sends James into the overgrown gardens of the villa, to find the summer-house and breathe in his last, forbidden air of the poet Shelley. Something of the narrator who will take Silsbee's place, inhabits him. He yearns for the letters and manuscripts his 'Juliana' hoards; and he plucks a flower, a blue columbine with leaves dust-speckled from the storm the trespasser's carriage made, when it came to break into the peace of this quiet offshoot of Padua. He will create a garden for his Misses Bordereau, its fragrance obscuring the sham his tale must necessarily be. Overpowered by the glory of his herbaceous prose, readers will suspend all disbelief, loyal to the hero in his attempt to secure the Aspern papers.

So the next construction may turn out well; yet the loveliness of this place overcomes everything. James hardly cares whether passion did take place between the poet and his wife's stepsister, Claire. Yet it *does* matter: the faint shimmer of the *Golden Bowl* hangs in the air; the difficulties and complications, the lies-behind-the-lies which must accompany a single meeting in an inn between lovers, make the Master stumble, as he traces the path to the summerhouse and stands listening for the scratch of the poet's pen. It does matter; and he feels, here and now, that it did take place

– and the last great book he will write floats from his imagination again, to await its time. For now, the transformed account of the destiny of a poetic archive is after all only a tale: and Miss Clairmont was known as the lover of Byron, not Shelley. 'I need an American Byron,' James murmurs, as the sun sinks low in the sky and he thinks he hears the first owl-call notes Shelley fluted by the castle walls, to amuse Claire's little daughter Allegra when she was brought out from Venice and stayed those few happy weeks with her mother here. 'An American Byron and an American Miss Clairmont' – the words sound, out in the garden as the roles are fixed, immutable, on the pages left behind at Palazzo Barbaro.

For a moment, as a curtain is pulled aside at a servant's window, and the hour of sleep in the heat of the afternoon ends, James knows himself a murderer, willing the deaths of Edward Silsbee, Shelley scholar, bore; and the vulgar Paula with the unpronounceable Hungarian name, niece of the misguided Claire. Without them, the true story of the woman who lived with the two greatest poets of the Romantic age could be told; of her resistance to the man who came as a lodger and waited like a vulture for her end; and of her foolish kindness to her niece and – so Lee Hamilton had said, for the details of Miss Clairmont's will had been the gossip of Florence for a time – her great-niece, a child even more unappealing than her mother. The child would inherit all.

It is time to return to Mrs Curtis, to the Palazzo the Boston-Venetians bought a short while ago and which they will repair and cherish. Mrs Gardner, with her long rope of pearls and her exigent demands for letters from the great writer, these plucked by her own hand from the oyster her Master declares himself, in all his desire for privacy, to be – Mrs Gardner will build her own Florentine palace back home, to dazzle Americans and impress the world. James feels more at home with Mr and Mrs Curtis than he ever did with Mrs Gardner.

But before he goes, he must walk to the window on the ground floor of I Cappucini and look in. Vines brush his face, it is shady, even appears to be growing dark, here in the house where the faded wall panels of ruby damask are heavily ornamented with oval portraits, all Italian noblemen and women, as James notes, and all of whom must by now be dead. An air of death emanates from the room, from sofas in cretonne and patterned silks long neglected, from mirrors pocked and marked with the onset of great age. That Claire was here once, surely cannot be true! – that she breathed this air of desuetude and lived to shine and dive between the man and wife she so freely put asunder! – that Shelley, who fled constraint whenever it came upon him, stayed contentedly here, first with Claire and her little daughter alone, then with poor Mary, who wept for her dead child Clara, killed by the discomforts of the journey her husband had made her undertake – none of this can be possible. There is no memory of life here; not a breath, even, of the wind that must have blown through Este on August nights, refreshing the poet and his wife and lover, and tantalising them in turn. The years of openness and hope and freedom they lived through have all gone; but James prefers the present, for all the signs of an increasing commercialism and rush in the world. It comes to him that Jeffrey Aspern is a Victorian gentleman dressed as a Romantic poet, and is as near as James will venture to the spirit of radicalism and free love.

He turns from the disappointing window and begins his trek across the overgrown garden. This is where he sees her – though she might be a tangled root, a pale fibre emerging from the tall shrubbery long left unpruned. A child, pale and fair; even in the fading light with a strong blue gaze and cheeks soft and creamy as the last flowers wilting on unwatered plants. He knows somehow she is Allegra: she is the symbol of that spirit of love and rebellion which blew through Europe and then went under, sat on by the new piety and hypocritical self-esteem of its successors. She was soon gone, too soon to know the dashing of the fine hopes of her parents or her adoptive uncle, Shelley, or of the war in Greece where Byron died. But here – now – she stands and then fades as evening intensifies and stars appear in the sky.

The carriage makes its way to Padua where the distinguished passenger will spend the night before going on to Venice in the morning. There, Alberto will meet him and he will leave land for water, having made his pledge to himself that his tale, so perceptive and original, shall remain the story of an American Byron; and an American Miss Clairmont, too. Almost as soon as the gondola begins its long glide towards the Piazza San Marco – where James will buy flowers for Mrs Curtis, lilies and roses, nothing wild as the untended blooms in the lost garden of I Cappucini – he starts to think of the letter – light and without reference to the overblown sentiments he had detected in her last missive – which he will write to Miss Woolson in Florence as soon as he's ensconced at home again, in the cosy grandeur of the Barbaro. 'The strange things that the American female does! – as witness the terrible Mrs Sherwood,' he pens later that day, when he has lunched with the Curtises and admired their plans for statuary to be imported from Ravenna. 'She invited me (and some others) to dine with her in London last summer, and then wrote a fearful letter about it (I having gone, all unconscious) to the American journals, which she afterwards sent me as if I should be delighted to see it.'

Fenimore will appreciate the awfulness of Mrs Sherwood, James knows. Nothing should be made public that is the domain of private life: they both agree on this. But he has to confess to suffering a pang, in his researches into his models for Miss Bordereau and Aspern in *The Aspern Papers*, Claire Clairmont and her long-dead lover, Shelley, that her secret letters to the poet at this period, sent to the Poste Restante at Pisa, had been addressed to a 'Joe James'. Something in Henry wishes he could be Joe. It is impossible, somehow, to imagine Shelley writing so careful a letter as James, who seals the envelope now with a sigh. The letter is about to be despatched to poor dear Fenimore, to the woman who loves him: a letter full of evasion and jokes.

# GEORGINA
## FLORENCE, 1876

We walked quickly, the child always a few steps
ahead, and as we came into the Piazza del Duomo
I saw she was leading me to the very centre of the city
and that we would go down into the crookedest maze
of alleyways and tenements, the area Julia will not let
me enter, for fear we are held up and are relieved
of our money and the other thing neither Julia nor
Mama will spell out, though Aunt is always ready to
talk of the 'unnecessary value put on virginity'.

This is the Via de Calzaioli, and the street and its
tributaries of filth and slime must have known many
murders. But the child Allegra, who walks here as if
in an arcade lined with glass-fronted shops, so proudly
does she go, pays no attention to the beggars and
hunchbacks and hideously deformed children who
press in on us; and soon, leaving the city's walls, we
are crossing a great river and find ourselves carried
downstream on a punt, heading – as I know because
she has promised me this a hundred times – for the
town in the sea where her father lives with his wolf
and his peacocks.

It begins to rain; but still the old man pushes his
pole down into the mud and soon I see Venice as it
has been shown me at home by Aunt Claire, when

she is in a good mood and the creditors have given her another month before they try to evict us all from the house. Our boat is now a gondola, one of the grandest in Venice, Allegra assures me, as it is her Papa's, and belongs to the Palazzo Mocenigo where he lives. I see the Doges' Palace, striped pink and white. There are other grand gondolas on this great canal, and some of the ladies and gentlemen disembark, handed up flights of steps that are covered with weed. Some of the boatmen are singing; they cluster round us when they see Allegra because she is so beautiful and – maybe – they know she is the daughter of the Lord who makes a scandal from his life and writes cantos all day long.

All I know of Lord Byron is that he used curling papers. Captain Silsbee heard that one day when he was up seeing Aunt. 'Don't tell anyone,' Byron had said. 'I'm as proud of my curls as any girl.' Aunt does love to tell him these things: quite different from the time Mr Graham was there and he asked Aunt about Lord Byron and she went very serious and spoke in a hushed tone. 'In 1815 when I was a very young girl,' Aunt said to Mr Graham, 'Byron was the rage. I was young, and vain and poor. He was so famous that people, and especially young people, hardly considered him a man at all, but rather as a god. The result you know. I am too old now to play with any mock repentance.'

So I'm to meet the man with lustrous dark curls, the man so famous he is seen as a god. Or so I believe, until Allegra turns to me and I see she stares at the houses on the other side of the canal from the Mocenigo. 'I shall find my mother here,' Allegra says. 'Shelley brings her and we go to a garden in the country, at Este.'

But before I could go to the garden at Este with my new friend Allegra, I was caught as I was running away in the Ca de' Calzaioli by Julia and Mama and the Captain all together. And I was brought back here to live as a prisoner until it is decided that I can be trusted once more to leave the house.

Allegra is not here any more, I have no one to play with or to entertain me. But today, just as the hot weather becomes unbearable for Aunt and she announces she must now, whatever the cost, go up to Fiesole, a new visitor appears. He is very old and very tall, and he insists on being lodged, as 'Miss Clairmont's oldest friend', in the dining-room, where Paula and Julia had to place a bed. His name is Mr Trelawny; and he will not be parted from a box that he says is full of Shelley's bones.

# HENRY
## DE VERE GARDENS, LONDON, 1887

It is July, and dark trees stand in the streets of Kensington, where Henry James has found a flat perfectly suited to his needs. There can be 'no Mrs HJ' ensconced here at no. 34 De Vere Gardens – this cry, emitted when house-hunting a year back and thus (falsely) assumed by his friends to be contemplating marriage, drove him from the possibility of a house to this fourth-floor redoubt. There can be nothing more (and nothing better) than a bachelor existence amounting quite simply to more of the same. There are friends in the vicinity, all of them aware of the Master's requirements: silence, privacy, and as much socialising to anguish over afterwards as his diary can fulfil.

There had been further intimations, before leaving Venice, of a love on Miss Woolson's part; a love which, regrettably, is learning more and more to speak its name. The letter written by Fenimore on realising that her evasive friend would not return to I Brichieri in Florence is plangent: this is the only word James could give to it. Nights at the Palazzo Barbaro had passed in extreme discomfort, with Fenimore's nearly-declared proposal of matrimony floating round the great room in the small hours, merely to be met with round-mouthed astonishment, even hilarity, by the ceiling's painted nymphs. It was unfortunate, too, that James's friend, the writer Paul Bourget, an expert on the cosmopolitan life of Florence, Venice and Rome and an almost-too-enjoyable gossip, had told of a recent scandal too engaging for the Master not to use. This story – of an adulterous elder sister who so shocked her younger sibling by her improper conduct that the latter went out in search of a good American husband, only to find her proposal turned down: the result, for the pure younger sister, was suicide – had haunted James, under his pink mosquito net. It had altogether grown too hot in Venice. By early June, it had been high time to return to the well-bred gloom of De Vere Gardens, away from poor Fenimore and what appeared to him as her unreasonable demands.

James's story, founded on the tale of the 'bad' sister and the good, will show him, once it is completed and published, as holder of a new code of tolerance, both for himself and for the times, for out of the two his sympathy is with the immoral woman. He actually disapproves of the younger and purer – and this, when Fenimore reads it, will surely demonstrate the new worldliness of the American she had hoped to make her husband. Even if she is not, Henry is acclimatised to the new spirit of lax behaviour. He turns a blind eye – even chuckles at – the scrapes and assignations of his cosmopolitan contemporaries. Surely – though he knows this is improbable in the extreme – Miss Woolson will learn from his tale that the once puritan author she woos so ardently is now – in theory if not in practice – a man of the world.

Henry James takes his cane, glances at his reflection

in the long panel of mirror set in the dark mahogany cupboard in his dressing-room, and goes out onto the landing of the fourth floor to await the lift. It comes up to him, noisy and obedient as a large dog, at his summons, and folds him neatly in its metallic arms. Here, he reflects as the cage carries him at a sedate pace to the hall, the porter in his three-sided box and the well-scrubbed steps leading to the leafy street, no one – and least of all Miss Woolson – knows where he is. He wishes, almost, that he could live in the lift, and be transported day and night from one floor of fiction to the next. Then, there could be no interruptions. But there is business to attend to; and he knows matters will improve when he has performed his task; even if, as most would remark on hearing it, the job in hand seems not to be onerous. For James holds a letter – a new letter, arrived this morning, which is as yet unopened; and which he must (though the day is destroyed by this knowledge of a duty owed to his friend, and the night before, with its peaceful sleep in the oldest-named street of English origin, De Vere, is as far distant now as another age) – he must, out in the anonymity of Hyde Park, quietly read. The postage stamp is Swiss. This must be where she'd gone to, poor Fenimore, when her companion, Henry, failed to return from Venice to sit on the terrace at I Brichieri and make love to Florence, stretched out below. Fenimore had clearly gone to Switzerland.

The last letter had been bad enough. Before putting the last touches to *The Aspern Papers*, James had made an ending that was an unmistakable declaration of his priorities. Miss Tina, the sad, dim, fifty-year-old niece of

Aspern's Juliana, shows her desire to marry the narrator, the Silsbee James both hates and sympathises with. In return for his acquiescence the younger Miss Bordereau will allow him ownership of the Aspern papers. But the narrator, James/Silsbee, for all his longing for those letters and papers, last relics of a great poet and his age, must refuse. James's tale concludes with the rejection of Miss Tina's offer; and with her burning the letters, one by one. The Master groans aloud when he thinks of it, already sent to Aldrich at *Atlantic Monthly* a fortnight ago and prepared for serialisation in three parts the following year. When Fenimore sees it, won't she –? But there is a letter in James's hand, and he makes for Kensington Gardens and the peace of the old palace there, in order to know the worst. There is no reason to suppose Fenimore has returned to her old reticent self (she had been so charming then, her deafness contributing to the unassuming air she gave out). No reason at all. And now, as the Master pauses by a bench at the side of the ornamental garden and bends to wipe a row of small rain puddles from the painted wood, he knows in his heart that this latest missive will embarrass him entirely.

'Of course, he might have conjectured that Constance Fenimore Woolson, novelist and teller of tales also, would have read Rousseau's novel about the unconsummated love of a master and pupil, *La Nouvelle Héloïse: Lettres de deux amants*. He might have recalled the passionate love and ensuing separation of Julie and her tutor St Preux. It had been the most romantic story of its time, more than a century ago by now. But love and passion, as James has to acknowledge, have a tediously timeless quality. Constance, in her letter, pictures herself hanging over the balcony of the Hôtel National – as Julie had done – and looking down at the placid waters of the lake. James knows, without dear Fenimore spelling it out – though she does!, she does! – that she was thinking not of Rousseau or St Preux, but of him. And, as he rises stiffly from the still-damp bench, the letter's recipient lets out another groan. Julie in *La Nouvelle Héloïse* had gone on to marry dutifully; a Baron Wolmar had been her husband, and all three, tutor, Baron and Julie lived virtuously ever after on the Baron's country estate. If only, James thinks as he strides – conscious of his present freedom at least – across Hyde Park on this lovely summer's day – if only Fenimore could wed a Baron Wolmar, that would be the end of all this. But nowadays a man was supposed to be as many men as a woman might want: mentor, lover and husband all in one.

# GEORGINA
## FLORENCE, 1876

The house is upside down and not for the first time, though the presence of Mr Trelawny makes it feel as if a wall of sea had burst in, bringing cockles and seaweed and what Mama and the Captain call the 'detritus' of all the lies they say he tells.

Trelawny is eighty-five years old and he wears no socks, so his feet, which are red and lumpy, look like slabs of meat for the dog, just stuck anyhow into shoes which are, like the rest of him, of a vast size. He has settled in the dining-room, and Julia is in despair, for she can no more get round him than she could a herd of bullocks. Trelawny shouts and jostles even in his sleep and if he believes a hand is reaching out to seize his treasure from him he lets out a dreadful bellow, this in turn bringing Aunt out of her room and onto the landing at the top of the stairs. It can only be good that Mama and Captain Silsbee are setting off for Naples later today – though if Aunt knew Silsbee's purpose, she would order him never to return here, I am sure. Silsbee wants to find out more about the dead baby he calls Elena Adelaide, registered in Naples and dying there a short time after. He hopes for more letters, I suppose, and to prise them from Aunt when he supplies the evidence he seeks. It is unseemly: there are fists coiled round papers and letters here – even bones, as the new visitor is happy to demonstrate. 'This is Shelley's jawbone,' says the strange old man each time I come into the stuffy little dining-room where Julia is not permitted to open the windows and let the fresh air in. 'The jawbone is white, Georgina, do you see? Whereas –' and he rummages in that precious box again, as if the devil had come in the night and made his relics vanish – 'the bone from the brow is quite black. This was due to the fire – the bonfire we made on the beach at Lerici, to cremate Shelley. His hair quite eaten away – ask your Aunt – it is unsurprising that the brow should be blackened by the fire, do you not agree?'

There is nothing I can say, when Trelawny talks and waves his bones about like this. I wish to ask him about Allegra – but I am too shy. He must have known the child, but he tells me, if I try to bring the subject up, that Aunt is the only woman he has ever loved. Despite the spouting of Shelley the Captain indulges in, it is with Trelawny that I feel myself truly in the exciting past Aunt enjoyed – before my mama was even born. I can almost see Shelley himself, so like a girl, as Trelawny likes to say over and over again – but nonetheless a girl all the women fall in love with, not least my Aunt Claire, whom Trelawny loved. There is much talk of love here now, and before he came, there was none at all.

For all that, he and Aunt quarrel violently when the old man goes up to see her and the flimsy stairs almost collapse under his pounding tread. I go after him, seconds later and quite unheard by either of them – 'Claire,' he's shouting before they've had time to exchange a courteous greeting, 'in my great age I have come to Italy for two things only. You know it, you are as stubborn, as dark and silver-spotted as a band of mercury – as you always were –'

'You come too late,' Aunt shouts back, while I'm thinking I know what one of old Trelawny's reasons is for his trip to Italy. He has come to arrange his burial site – I shall have to hear about the trees all over again. But I love Trelawny – and I don't mind following him up here, to listen to his tale of the seven cypresses and the ashes one more time. I don't want the old man to die, not yet – and he won't, strong and impatient as he is. Trelawny goes out to walk for hours along the Arno to get the air – even if his relics in our dining-room must be protected against any winds that might blow in.

'In the Protestant cemetery in Rome,' Trelawny thunders. 'With seven cypresses planted back in 'twenty-two. Claire, I shall be with Shelley and I trust you have made arrangements also. We are not young –' and with these words Trelawny pounds the table where Aunt writes her letters and takes her morning coffee.

'No, we are not young,' Aunt replies, when the sound of Trelawny's fist subsides and the canary Aunt keeps in a cage on her balcony is twittering away once more. 'This is why I cannot do as you ask, Edward. My eyes are so bad –' and, again, I feel I know Aunt's movement when she tries to describe the near-blindness which descends on her at times when she reads or tries to concentrate on documents and journals Silsbee brings up to her – 'it would be impossible for me to do, I fear.'

'You have had *fifty* years in which to write your memoirs of that time,' Trelawny says after a long pause, and this time he speaks very softly and the bird gives what sounds like a squawk of disapproval or alarm. 'I have tried without success to sell your Shelley letters, as you well know. You could dictate your memories, my dear Claire – is not your excellent niece Paula your amanuensis? Or –' and here my blood races and I turn by the closed door of the topmost room, ready to flee down the stairs – 'the delightful Georgina, who will do anything for you. Of this I am quite sure. She is your heir, is she not, my friend? Let her learn the secrets of the past: she has every interest in keeping them to herself.'

When Aunt laughs, she makes the sound Silsbee says must have entranced Shelley – and now I know Trelawny I can sense he loves the laugh as well – though Mama makes a face when she hears it. In fact, Mama can't bear hearing this laughter when Silsbee goes up there – even if Miss Clairmont, Constantia in Shelley's poems as the Captain has explained to me, is nearly as old now as our visitor, Trelawny. Laughter, like love – so the strange old man insists – never ages. But I know already, from Mama's shrewd, worried look and the tears I hear her shed sometimes at night when the Captain is out at dinner in Florence, that both laughter and love may turn to ashes faster than the bodies burned on the beach at Lerici.

'You want my memories from me so you can add them to your own,' Aunt cries, and I realise her laughter had been mocking, there had been no love in it at all. 'To add to your "Recollections" or your "Record" – leave me mine.'

And before I have had time to reach the landing below, Aunt's door is pulled open, almost wrenched off its hinges by Trelawny, and he is standing roaring just above me, like the monster in my worst nightmare. 'I have a right to see the letters you aim to sell,' he says, on one of these quiet notes that are so disconcerting after all the shouting and pounding. 'Show them to me, Claire.'

'Only if you give me mine back,' Aunt says in the coldest voice I have ever heard her use. And she closes the door on Trelawny, who stays up there a full minute, like a sailor stranded in the crow's nest of a ship, looking bewildered and uncertain out to sea.

# HENRY
## LONDON, JULY 1887

'I could not, for a bundle of tattered papers, marry a ridiculous, pathetic, provincial old woman.' As Henry James makes his way along the southern fringe of Hyde Park – the trees are heavy with their July leaves, they have outworn the freshly minted quality for which arboreal glories, as much as young women, must be admired – he shrinks from the comparisons and analogies poor Constance Fenimore Woolson will make, when reading his new masterpiece, due to appear shortly in *Atlantic Monthly*. How can Fenimore fail to see herself as Miss Tina? – how can he ever make amends for his portrait of a spinster brought briefly to life by the advent of a mysterious bachelor in the denuded palace she shares with her antediluvian aunt, and then abandoned, returned to a dim old age? Had he not, like the narrator devoted to the acquisition of the Aspern papers, led her on in a myriad cruel, subtle ways? Indeed, on the occasion of Fenimore's first visit to Venice after making the acquaintance of the Master, hadn't he taken her on heady gondola rides, stood long in the Accademia before the great works of art which gave him each time fresh inspiration: – had he not looked sideways, in that unmistakable manner of his when intrigued and charmed by a new friend, at Miss Woolson, as if to express complicity in the experience of the higher recognition of great art? Then, physical similarity to Miss Tina apart, poor Fenimore has no letters to use as a bargaining tool. She must know that when she reads the novella, she will weep at her own presumption in expecting a reciprocal affection from James – she has no trove of Romantic jewels, after all, no mementoes of a new Europe bursting forth from the pens of her past lovers – she is, quite simply, Miss Woolson. 'I gave her no cause,' James murmurs, as he hails a cab and gives the address in Cheapside of the restaurant where he will lunch with an old friend of the Duveneck family: there will be much talk of Bellosguardo and the past year's Florence gossip to discuss. Yet, 'I gave her no cause,' he repeats the phrase under his breath in the horse-drawn vehicle in its slow clop towards the promise of fresh fish in the carefully selected eating-place (he will try the Dover sole, magnificently on the bone when brought to the table, then filleted – so he hopes – with great dexterity by a young waiter with the sleek black hair of the Palazzo Barbaro's Alberto). As 'I gave her no cause' sounds in his mind a third time, James knows the words to be not his, but those of the narrator of the Aspern papers, the publishing scoundrel, the very man he has spent so agonisingly long attempting not to be. Of course! – the dissembling, cunning purloiner of old Miss Bordereau's treasure gives away his creator as much as himself with his protestation of innocence. Both he – a common burglar, a man so greedy for the papers once ruffled by the breath of genius that he will court an old maid and ransack a private chamber – and the author of his unfortunate character, are one and the same man, guilty in the eyes of all good and charitable beings in this world. Letters or no letters, James has encouraged Fenimore to love him and to anticipate a return of that love.

And, as the horrible thought comes to him that James's own letters and hers make up for him a treasure as vital to obtain as those of the great poet Jeffrey Aspern had been for his ardent scholar, he groans aloud in the hackney cab, and the driver turns to bend down from his seat to look in at him there. The irony does not escape James, that this is hardly the time to become ill – to lose consciousness even, as he feels himself on the brink of doing. To be found with Fenimore's incriminating letter in his pocket! – and, as he remembers other occasions, the trip in the gondola for instance, with Alberto to search for the unfashionable district where he would place his substitute for Miss Clairmont and her niece: hadn't he also just received a letter from Fenimore then? He groans aloud at the suppositions that inevitably will be made when the revelation of Henry James's peculiar habit is in the public domain: James – the Master – unable to travel abroad without a missive from his lover on his person! Beatrice to his Dante. So great is the agony of his passenger that the driver pulls in to the side of the busy road and reins in until the old geezer (a good forty-five in the cabbie's opinion, surely he's been taking his pleasures too seriously) appears well enough to continue the journey. 'You said Sweetings, guv?' the man shouts down from the box. But he is answered with a shake of the head and a shudder. 'Near Sweetings,' comes the pained directive. But there are literary connotations to the word, and James wishes it had not been mentioned. For Shakespeare it was, he who is greater even than Jeffrey Aspern, who had sadistically provided the hidden implications. 'Journeys end in lovers' meetings.' From *Twelfth Night*, of course, that is it. James makes a pretence of quoting the lines, to himself.

But he arrives in Cheapside an unhappy – even a rattled – man. There must be no more letters from Fenimore, especially ones like this one, where she compares herself and Henry to the lovers in *La Nouvelle Héloïse*.

The restaurant selected for luncheon is one which succeeds in looking full when in fact there is almost no one there. Brass pots with large ferns and dark embossed Turkish screens obscure a true view of seating arrangements; and mirrors, set at unexpected angles, do the rest. A hum of apparently contented diners emanates from hidden corners, and today, as regular clients have come to expect, little more than the silver chime of a falling fork or the bustle of a too quickly folded napkin can be heard above the sound of discreet conversation.

Henry James is seated at a table near the door: from here he will have the opportunity of recognising his guest, picking out by long familiarity with the expatriate's manner of walking, clothing himself and holding his head, the obvious candidate for luncheon companion and friend of the Duvenecks. However camouflaged in English tweeds, the American-Florentine awaited by James will have no need to suffer the humiliation of the dreadful uncertain pause, on behalf of head waiter and, in this case – for they have not met before – of genial host. James will not need to hesitate. He will know his man.

There are, however, lacunae, faux pas, even in the best of restaurants; and it so happens, due perhaps to an unacknowledged desire on the part of the sleek black-haired waiter (indeed, the famous author had remembered him, and there was after all a strong resemblance to Alberto, conductor of the Stygian gondola, guide to the deepest fantasies and dreams a writer can entertain, those of finding the house, canal, lake or lagoon where he can safely place his characters) – due to an unconscious wish to hurry up the meal, possibly in order to spend time, if this should be suggested, of an agreeable and post-prandial nature with the great man – that entirely the wrong guest is ushered to Mr James's table. Before there is a chance of waving away the impostor – as it were – or of alerting the double of Alberto, at least, of his cardinal mistake, Henry James is confronted by a man who is both a total stranger to him and at the same time horribly familiar. 'There is a table in the name of Buxton Forman,' the stranger says; he is tall and whiskered and he looks down at the seated James as if at a child amusing itself by the side of an ornamental pool: he might topple the hapless guest into the water, his belligerent stance suggests, with the slightest movement of his huge frame. 'Ah yes, Captain Silsbee,' the penitent – and now hideously-unlike Alberto – waiter declares; and James notes there is no glance of apology in his direction. 'This way please – Mr Buxton Forman awaits you.' So, with a bow that marks this guest out as welcome in a mysterious way that Mr James is not, the waiter leads the new arrival to a table on a higher level – but well within earshot, as the author notes. Now at last – and with the execrable timing for which he will not be forgiven throughout the meal – the awaited guest is to be seen coming through the door. The waiter returns, greets the friend of the Duvenecks, shows him to his seat at Mr James's table. As if it was all one to him! – so James thinks later, his rage and astonishment still clamouring inside him. As if it could have been endurable, to share food and drink with Silsbee! – as if, most appallingly of all, there was little to distinguish between the elegant American, pillar of Florentine society, who now sits with the Master and toys nervously with a fluted glass, and a soapless, stanza-spouting bore.

As might have been expected, this is not all that has to be put up with by the author: indeed, on later reflection, the only conclusion that could be arrived at was one of rueful recognition, that each stab in the vicinity of the heart received in the course of that interminable luncheon served to underline the worst fears and anxieties of the occupation – vocation – or, as James now gloomily accepts, simply trade, of a writer. The first – and some would say the most fearsome – experience is to hear words or witness actions earlier conceived as part of a private fiction (and still, in the case of *The Aspern Papers*, unpublished) mouthed or performed by a person in real life. Worst after this – for James hears Silsbee now, his voice is loud from years of declaiming his hero, Shelley – trumpeting his late successes to Mr Forman and another at his table – is the confirmation, in the triumphant enactment of these scenes, of exactly the depravity the writer had imagined for him. A real man – Silsbee – transformed to James's narrator returns as the ghastly spectre of Silsbee again. And his boasts – of stealing poor Miss Clairmont's carefully hoarded treasure, in this case Shelley's manuscript book, no less – bring a redness and heat to James's cheeks that prompt the kind friend of the Duvenecks to ask if all is well with him. How could the real Silsbee know that his counterpart in James's brief work would go as far as theft, to accomplish his aims? – this is all James can murmur to himself, as the bewildered cosmopolite sips his wine and wonders secretly if he should not leave the restaurant and return to his hotel.

'You don't reckon with my smartness,' Silsbee says loudly and clearly – and it appears to James that the whole place, with its unascertainable number of patrons, falls silent and hangs on the scoundrel's words. 'I had the niece Paula – gentlemen, you will forgive the expression, I do sincerely trust, but *having* is all this fine story is about – and ensured this was my path to having the jewel of the Shelley collection for myself. I would send the child up for it – Paula's child, you know. She brought me down the letters I required, usually – but in this case, with the dark, treacherous Claire – that is Miss Clairmont, my friends, or was: the mistress of Byron and Shelley both – with Claire there was often no way of knowing, as she slept, whether she did not really stay awake. Her eyes were always seen to be open – that was the uncomfortable truth of it all. And Paula herself – it took some "having" to persuade her, I can vouchsafe – was the only one who could take the treasure from the cupboard without alarming or otherwise disturbing her dear aunt.'

James rises; he seems on the point of apoplexy. The whole scene, written by him, unrolls before his eyes: the tiptoeing thief, the waking Miss Bordereau, the 'Juliana' whose proof of Aspern's love is stolen from her. The room turns and dances, before the author's eyes. 'No, it is nothing – someone I thought I recognised.' He resumes his seat, with difficulty. Now, he must exhibit the perfect manners expected of him by this dear, cherished friend of the Duvenecks.

'I have been meaning to ask you for news of Miss Woolson,' the dry, quiet American says, as a succession of plates is placed before them. 'We heard she was ill, recently – I do so hope she has recovered both her spirits and her health?'

'Ah, Fenimore,' James says, numb with the effort of control, open only to the bragging of Silsbee as it echoes amongst the potted ferns and tall screens of the restaurant. 'I have not heard very lately –'

'Constance,' says the dry man, who gives a dry laugh in acknowledgement of what he assumes to be Henry James's wit. 'I have always heard Miss Woolson referred to as Constance.'

Henry James fidgets at the table and a fork clatters to the floor. His inner defences are breached: he knows his reason, at last, for veering from Miss Woolson's name. The artist's muse, the love of his life – James cannot permit his old 'acquaintance', as he gives out Miss Woolson to be, the luxury of such a title.

'Shelley's verses to his Constantia,' Silsbee roars from his concealed table on the mezzanine. And James, throat choked, shakes his head and says it's just a joke between them, he has always addressed Miss Woolson as Fenimore.

# GEORGINA
## FLORENCE, 1876

Mr Trelawny had a child, by the daughter of the
Greek chief Odysseus, and she died, like Allegra,
very young, her coffin held up days in Corfu while
her mother's family waited on the island of Zante
to reclaim their child. Mr Trelawny tells me stories
so sad anyone would cry – but it is he, despite
Julia standing in the doorway of the musty little
dining-room, ready with a white handkerchief to
begin sobbing at a tale of lost love and dead children
– he who does the crying. I can hear the wind in
the pines on the Welsh mountains he tells me of,
and I can see the great cave where he hid with the
Greek chief on Mount Parnassus, and I walk up to
Lord Byron dead – but still I don't cry, and nor does
Julia. The stories sound like words learnt by heart
– but Mama says none of it is true and Aunt looks
sceptical. Whichever way you hear the extraordinary
life-histories of Edward Trelawny, you know they may
be learnt by heart but he has lost his a long time ago.
To Claire – to the 'dark, subtle, treacherous' aunt I
have – so he tells me, and he says he had loved his
daughters Lateitia and Zella, after Claire they were
all that mattered to him in the world. Then he cries
again, into a bandanna that is big enough to cover a

map of all the places he has travelled and the seas and rivers he has swum. Julia still stands there, dry-eyed.

One determination I have I can confide to Trelawny, because of all his faults, a lacking of sympathy is not one. Children – especially daughters – are Trelawny's strongest suit. He looks at me very seriously when I say I used to see Allegra and play with her, the blue-eyed daughter of Lord Byron and my aunt Claire. He nods, and asks why I've stopped meeting this new friend, who would stand on the landing at any time of the night or day and then take my hand and suggest running away together, to see her mama when she was young, and be rescued from the grim convent where she had been sent. 'Allegra is at the convent now,' I say to Trelawny and we sit at the dining-table on the hard chairs with backs shaped like lyres, as if we are plotting a conspiracy to bring her back. 'Ah yes, the convent in the marshes of Romagna,' Trelawny says – and now Julia does burst out sobbing by the door and turns to go back to the kitchen, immediately reappearing with a dish of figs. 'You know,' Trelawny says when we have bitten into the silky strands inside the fig and, in Trelawny's case, the fruit has exploded all over his mouth, making him look as if he's been shot with one of the muskets he tells us about, 'you do know that it's better all round if Allegra stays there in the convent, don't you? The nuns are kind, and she is secure there. Her father is no longer in Venice – or Ravenna –' 'No,' I say, and I remember the winter carnival at Ravenna I read about in one of the letters in the cupboard in Aunt's room upstairs: Allegra had run out in the snow with her father's mistress Teresa and they had thrown confetti which landed like red and blue spots of blood on the snow as it fell and melted quickly. 'Allegra would like to go back to the palace her father had there,' I say. 'The war will be over soon, won't it?' And we both fall silent, while I think how kind it is of Trelawny to pretend we're in those years so long ago, when Claire was young and Allegra was still alive, praying to the Madonna and forgetting her mother with each day that passed. But it's sad, at the same time; and Trelawny is snorting into his great cloth again. I can tell, though, from the way he tries to pull his huge age and weight into an upright position on the dainty chair, that he thinks it's time the game was over.

'Georgina,' Trelawny says, and I see he is really serious this time and that we are alone in the stifling little room with the red embossed wallpaper I have grown to hate. 'Georgina, it is important that you help me persuade your aunt that Allegra really is dead. She doesn't believe it, you know.'

Of course I know, I feel like saying, with some of the sharp tongue Claire uses when she's in the mood. Both Mama and I have inherited it. Of course I can only see Allegra because Aunt believes she didn't die – she thinks it was all a trick played on her by Byron to lose the irritation the mother of his adored daughter had become.

'She *was* enchanting,' says Trelawny – and for a moment I know he's seeing Allegra too, just as I used to do.

I fear Trelawny will have another of his violent quarrels with Aunt, unless she agrees with everything he says. I had promised him I'd talk to her about the death of Allegra – but I didn't dare, for I don't want to lose my chance of imagining the child again, with her fair hair, and the imperious way she has of ordering her world around. 'Shelley loved little Alba so,' Aunt says sometimes, when she speaks of the past and her eyes drop half-shut, which is as far as they'll ever go.

We are walking along, Trelawny and I, and the old pirate at eighty years old or more goes faster than I can run. I feel I'm in a dream, as is so often the case, with a curtain between the real world, where I am expected to 'pursue my education' – this means, when Aunt says it, that she is thinking hard about selling Shelley, and that another letter saying she is asking too much has arrived in the post today – and the world of dreams I have learned to enter through the letters and diaries she doesn't really want to let go. What is so unexpected just now, so unlike the usual pattern of dream and awakening, is the fact that reality has turned to dream, not the other way around.

Trelawny and the woman he once loved had a great fight last night, as I had foreseen they would. I waited by Aunt's room to hear it out, and by the time Trelawny shouted and banged his fist down three times on her flimsy table, I knew the old man meant what he said. 'I'll go to Bagnocavallo, Claire,' came the voice he liked to boast had been heard in the Agora at Athens when he declaimed at the mouth of Odysseus's cave on Mount Parnassus. 'I'll bring you evidence myself of Allegra's death. Then this foolish obsession will leave you – you'll be the better for it, and so will we all.'

'No, Edward.' I clenched my teeth when I heard Aunt talk like that: she has no notion, I suppose, of the obstinacy and anger she betrays when she answers in this way. But then Mr Silsbee, who may be half in love with her himself as Mama says he is, reminds us each time of the long years in Russia, when Aunt suffered so as a governess, and of all the privations she has endured. Even when Shelley's legacy came through, she invested it badly, so Mama reminds him, buying a box at Covent Garden and losing hand over fist as soon as the purchase took place.

'The nuns will have a record of the death of the child,' Trelawny said and I couldn't help admiring him for his insistence as I stood there in the hot air of a July evening, eavesdropping by the window open on the stairs.

'I could go myself,' Aunt said in a thoughtful voice; and I knew she was thinking of long-ago escapades, the kind of mad plan people like Shelley and Byron had in those days. And I am expected to study them!

'You almost went to Bagnocavallo,' Trelawny said, and his voice was gentle again. 'I heard of your courage, Claire –'

'I became a Catholic,' Aunt said – and now for the first time I understood why Aunt goes to Mass when Mama says none of the Clairmont family were brought up as papists. I've noticed that she and the Captain talk a lot about Aunt's coming death. Will she have a full Catholic burial?, they say to each other. Who will pay for it?

I have understood that Aunt converted to Catholicism purely in order to try and rescue her daughter from the convent at Bagnocavallo. 'It was such a clever idea,' Aunt said to Trelawny, but softer now so I could barely hear. 'I was to be a pensionnaire at San Giovanni and so find a way of being with poor little Allegra. After a while she would trust me enough to go outside the convent walls with me and we would both be free.' Then Aunt started to cry – the subject of Allegra is always the one to set her off. I could hear Trelawny whisper kind things to Aunt – and then, ashamed to be listening in on the old friends, I ran down the stairs and shut myself in my room.

So you could say the fight ended in reconciliation. But it's never like that with Claire, and not, as I recognise, with Trelawny either. He has good reason for wanting to find proof of Allegra's death which will end Aunt's mania. She'll dictate some more memories to him, he'll make another book out of them. He has taken me along almost absent-mindedly. He'll go on at my Aunt until she accepts that it wasn't, as she insists on believing, a goat that Lord Byron put in a coffin from Leghorn to foggy England. It was his poor little daughter, Allegra. Trelawny has memories of his own child by the Greek chieftain's daughter, perhaps. But I don't like to think of that, because it's easy to believe this great ogre of a man cares only for himself, when it comes down to it.

So I really am going to Bagnocavallo, where Allegra died of the typhoid all those years ago. I may even see her – though I don't think so somehow: Trelawny banishes ghosts by reason of his size and his certainty that he belongs in the real world. The nuns who cared for Allegra may have died too by now, of course; and in that case Trelawny may find it hard to obtain the proof he needs. But knowing the man, he will come back with a memento, even if the confirmation of Allegra's death in the convent is nowhere to be found. As for the infant Elena Adelaide, whose birth Silsbee 'discovered' in the city in the south, Trelawny gave only one of his long, contemptuous grunts when the Captain had the temerity to bring the subject up.

Bagnocavallo is about twelve miles from Ravenna. Trelawny has taken a carriage from the outskirts of Florence as it will save money, but it will cost him a good deal and I know he must be set on banishing this bee from Aunt's bonnet, as he is fond of putting it.

The first thing I see is the walls and towers of the town, and I see the land is very cultivated with vines. Spinach grows in long peasant allotments, but it is lank and gone to seed at this time of year and I train my eyes on the white, dusty road so as not to have to think of death and Allegra when I see dying plants and the like. I am hot and thirsty, and Trelawny has fallen into one of his silences. I begin to wish I hadn't come after all to the convent where my friend learnt discipline: she, who had been as wild and free as a child can be when it is spoilt and ignored by turns. My heart bleeds for her. Once – after I had been reading a letter in Claire's room from someone unknown to Aunt (so I believe) describing the pine forests outside Ravenna where Allegra and Teresa Guccioli would go in hot weather – she led me all the way to the sea, beyond the pines where the wind turns cool even in the fiercest summer weather. I know she loved to bowl along, under those great trees: what can it have been like for her, to be confined to the small convent garden, with its neat rows of forget-me-nots, and the marigolds so bright an orange that they hurt the eye? What did Allegra feel as she walked the long, bare passages of San Giovanni and stopped at each plaster saint, in painted robes, secure in its alcove in the walls?

There is a sadness and a greyness here, even if the sun pushes into the small courtyard: in the cloister it is dank, and even almost cold. I remember the anguished letters Aunt wrote to Byron, begging him to remove his daughter from the nuns; and the scrawled missives to friends where Claire describes the only heat the sad Allegra will ever know at San Giovanni: a piece of smouldering charcoal in a glass, around which the child can cup her hands.

I have been left alone here quite a time, as Trelawny is with the Mother Superior and he has emerged from the chapel only once, to hand me a small box, shaped like a book and leather bound. Then he returned to his serious discussions; and after a while a nun of about fifty came and joined them, the chapel door closing behind her as she went silently in. Time passes very slowly here, even more slowly than it does at home, and I see why there are prayers so often and bells that ring to summon the nuns. They are Capuchins, the poorest order of them all. I feel the absolute absence of my friend: her vitality, her life all gone; and like Aunt I release my tears. But then the chapel door opens and the

Mother Superior and Trelawny come out, and the veiled nun behind them.

Back at home, the book that is a box with steel bands is opened and Trelawny lifts out a miniature portrait of Allegra and a lock of her hair, just the dark fairness I had imagined the gloomy convent walls would make it. I stare at the minute portrait – but the large eyes and smug expression of Allegra don't seem to me to belong to her at all. 'It is true,' says Trelawny, who seems relieved, after a day with the nuns, to have the company of Silsbee and Mama, just returned from Calabria, to listen to more of his 'records' and reminiscences, 'that the child Allegra's brain was found to be of a very great size, after her death. The loss of Byron's daughter was a loss to the world of an intellect which is hard yet to evaluate.'

And so, with Mama busy exchanging glances with the Captain, as if to say the old rascal is back to pontificating again, with his mixture of half-lies and truths, I am the one who is sent to the front door when a loud banging on the knocker finally interrupts Mr Trelawny's stream of recollections.

A man, not as old as Trelawny and paunchy like Silsbee but very swarthy and dark, stands on the doorstep. He bows and greets me as if I were a real young lady, met at a Court Ball. 'Please inform la Signorina Clairmont,' the stranger says, in clear, loud tones, 'that Signor Luigi Gatteschi pays her a visit here today.'

I must have stared at the caller, and my inability to move back in the doorway coincides with Mama stumping into the hall to see what all the fuss is about.

At the same time, Signor Gatteschi moves forward and tries to elbow past me. He repeats his name – and now Mr Trelawny and the Captain come out into the hall to examine the visitor. 'Please also inform Miss Clairmont,' says the stranger now in English, 'that I have –' and here he pauses, for he sees our surprise written on our faces – 'that Luigi Gatteschi is the possessor of a very good memory.'

# HENRY
## CLOUDS, WILTSHIRE, FEBRUARY 1888

Clouds is a house which exactly suits Henry James in this bleak winter, when 34 De Vere Gardens, in those hours when he is not working or pacing the large, light rooms, seems to promise only loneliness: dinner parties, gossip and the fear of a life subjected entirely, like that of Paul Overt in James's recent story 'The Lesson of the Master', to the demands of high art. William, Henry's brother, writes to him from across the Atlantic, expressing wonder at the output of Henry: tales, stories, novels at the short intervals a lack of family – or academic commitments, such as William's – can permit the author. Indeed, London life, for all its stale air and repetitive social occasions, is what Henry needs; and yet, on receiving an invitation to the country, he had been surprised to find he was eager to lose the consciousness of self – and of all the selves his fiction presses on him – in the company of the high-born, the influential, those who are politicians born and bred. There is perhaps another motive for Henry's welcome, in this dreary month, of the kind suggestion of Percy and Madeline Wyndham that he come for a few days to the house that is a pinnacle of the new movement in English design, Clouds at East Knoyle. The reason may be that there has been no letter for some time now, from Fenimore. He knows her to be in Oxford; and it would have been easy for them to communicate. But something must hold her back – her reticence, as he remembers, like her deafness, can intensify at certain moments – could she be offended with him? Should he have returned to I Brichieri, rather than lingering in Venice and indulging his love of real history over invention with that visit to Este? – does she feel, although he has once, recklessly, described her as a 'dear' and even an 'intimate', that she no longer means anything in his life? It has not occurred to Henry that he could himself have written to Fenimore, and the whole awkwardness could have been ended. Something about the memory of that dreadful luncheon in Cheapside, and the shocked comments of Mr Buxton Foreman, on sweeping out with his companion after the scoundrel Silsbee, that to seduce a woman without intention of marriage was an appalling way to behave – but to use her in order to acquire a valuable manuscript infinitely worse – had prevented James from writing even the briefest line to his old friend. That she would know in a scant number of months' time just how she had been taken advantage of – as Miss Tina in the gloomy precincts of the palazzo in Rio Marin had been both fascinated and courted by a man with literary passions and finally abandoned when her price for the letters was seen to be too high – so poor Fenimore had been at first toured and fêted by the Master, only to remain ungraciously ignored during all those lonely months in Bellosguardo last year. She had modelled for him – this is the only way he can perceive the trusting, passive stance of Miss Woolson in the lead-up to the writing of *The Aspern Papers* – and on completing the portrait, the artist had thrown his sitter in the street, recorded for posterity but discarded from his life. If this way of thinking appears at times excessively dramatic, James has only to remind himself of the fact that Fenimore, who travels with a thousand hampers, suitcases, baskets and parcels, from one rented house or flat to another, is known never to have thrown anything away. The James letters surely travel with her. Does he really need to add to the trove, transforming his modest friend into Miss Clairmont at the same time? The thought may be amusing, but it is not so far from the truth. The hideous coincidence revealed (to Henry's conscious mind at least) on the occasion of overhearing Silsbee, of Shelley's muse being addressed as Constantia, and Miss Woolson being Constance – coupled with the gloomy expectation of lifelong fidelity associated with the name in the first place – has successfully banished the possibility of writing to Fenimore, for quite some time at least.

Nonetheless, Henry feels the absence of her letters. Both physically: had there not been a pattern (or so it had come to appear) in the manner in which their recipient invariably found himself out in the world with one of Fenimore's most affectionate, not to say 'intimate' letters concealed about his person? Had the great author been, as vulgar parlance went, run over by a tram, what type of relationship would have been arrived at by policemen rifling through the pockets of the corpse's trousers or his Norfolk jacket? – and mentally: the thought brings an inevitable shudder, even a frisson of excitement; surely, on further examination by forensic experts, Fenimore's missives would be pronounced to be those of a woman confident of her love for the sadly deceased man, if not actually his fiancée. The anxiety occasioned, either on water in the Curtises' gondola or on foot in the teeming traffic of Kensington High Street, had, as James half admits to himself, provided an impetus to the fiction he would write later in the day.

So what is wrong with marriage, after all? Henry James descends from the first-class carriage of the train at Salisbury, wonders briefly if there is time to visit the Cathedral and decides against it when he sees the handsome conveyance sent to meet him – and steps up into a comfort of cushions and the anticipation of an interesting drive through beautiful countryside, to Clouds. He knows his hostess Madeline as a goddess of family life, a woman for whom the dubious word 'creative' could have been coined, an artist and a mother who lets her children roam free, the presiding spirit of the fine Philip Webb-designed house with its expanse of carpets and tapestries by Burne-Jones and William Morris. Here, as James has heard tell, is the perfect setting for a modern and fruitful marriage. Can this be a (submerged) reason for the eagerness to become a guest at Clouds? To witness all the benefits of a fulfilled and legally sanctioned union? James, as the landau turns into the drive of the mansion built with Percy Wyndham's undoubted fortune, has no wish to remind himself that he and Fenimore, should they wed, would be renters and not visionary builders or even owners: in London, would he wish for her in the careful spaces of De Vere Gardens, or she for him in dim, dingy Oxford lodgings? Would marriage for them

– and here Henry dismisses the subject from his mind as the dwindling size of his royalties returns to haunt him, and Fenimore's handsome advances along with them, appear on burgeoning sales sheets before his eyes – would marriage be tolerable, without a Clouds to sustain their fond visions of each other? Would he not – he cannot answer for dear Fenimore here – prefer in reality to be dead?

*Fragment of a letter from Henry James to William James, 20 February 1888*

I will get you to-day the fotos of A. Balfour & Morley.[1] I dined in company with the former & only one other man (2 other women) about a week ago; & was struck afresh with the degree to which in spite of his extremely pleasant, lazy and apparently sincere manner he is the type of latent aristocratic insolence and scorn, of the extremely refined & intellectual sort. He is extremely witty, & a master of persiflage & badinage &, at the same time is of the cold, ascetic and unfleshly type, not liking English sports & brutalities – only lawn-tennis, reading & conversation: purely virginal & cerebral. There is something painful to

[1] Arthur Balfour (1848–1930), philosopher and Conservative statesman, future prime minister (1902–3), was in 1887 fierce chief secretary for Ireland ('Bloody Balfour'). John Morley, MP, associated with Macmillan's when HJ began publishing with them, had been chief secretary for Ireland in 1886 in the Liberal government and in 1887 was important in the Round Table Conference on Irish policy.

me in seeing a man of his extremely fine intellectual quality associated so intensely with the purposes of all the dense & brutal clan – I mean, the stupid thousands of 'society', the cast of whose minds is in a measure the shame of the English race. *Aussi*, he today is the darling, the adored of London – they have never before had such a pure brain, & such a flexible wit (in talk at least – less so in the H. of Commons) at their service & *ils ne se connaissent plus*. I met yesterday, at a call, George Shaw-Lefevre, who apparently sincerely considers that Arthur Balfour is a deeply, coldly & deliberately *cruel* nature approaching the *infernal*: absolutely destitute of heart or sensibility. I spent 2 days, in the autumn, at a country house with B. & Wilfrid Blunt & have feared since that I shld. be called upon to testify in regard to that visit – what passed between them – Blunt's allegations having since made it historical. Blunt is a humourless madman & a very disagreeable person. Balfour I should think indeed a prodigy of amiable heartlessness. It all comes back to *race* – high Scotch Tory ancestry, lands & dominions. The lands, ancestry & Toryism give the insolence, & Scotland the *mind*[.]

This was the pronouncement of Henry James to his brother, on his fellow guests at Clouds. Another reason for his extreme dislike of Arthur Balfour can be deduced, however; for at dinner on the first day of the great writer's visit to the architect Philip Webb's masterpiece, the dreadful truth of the chief secretary for Ireland's secret addiction had been revealed. Balfour and the charming Lady Elcho – daughter of his hosts – are inveterate letter writers. Balfour confesses to having 'stupidly burnt' the last missive from Mary in which she enquires on the nature of his new Philosophical Work; and further badinage reveals that, for all the show of marital affection between Lord Elcho and his wife, a clearly amorous relationship exists, if only in the minds and hearts of Arthur and Mary, between the white crested sheets employed by the English nobility when confiding their inner thoughts and passions to paper. The openness and frank delight with which the epistolary lovers discussed their correspondence – and the indifference to high moral values exhibited by the woman generally considered to be a perfect specimen of her sex, Madeline Wyndham, in the face of such blatant referral to letters, had shocked Henry profoundly. He passed a bad night, despite the luxury of a Clouds bachelor's bedroom with all its simplicity: monastically white walls, Morris birds and foliage to give a glimpse of the Utopia attainable if Socialist ideals are realised; and hot water brought at an early hour by a housemaid who is, as Madeline had liked to emphasise to her distinguished guest at dinner the night before, housed in a special wing designed by Webb to provide as many comforts and conveniences as possible to the staff. The dinner, plain and sumptuous as the surroundings, had nevertheless provided acute indigestion, though it is probable that the altercation between Wilfrid Blunt, the poet and rebel, supporter of the Irish cause, and the ruthless, autocratic Balfour, had mixed acid into the blameless menu. James wakes dyspeptic and panicky: he can no longer remember exactly what crime Blunt had accused Balfour of – something to do with nationalist leaders in Ireland not sufficiently respected by the chief secretary – but he knows that the detestable Blunt, along with the icily insolent Balfour, are a good reason for finding an excuse to leave Clouds tomorrow, Sunday, if he can find a suitable one. This is not the restful experience that had been hoped for; nor, as James wryly acknowledges, has it proved an example of happy marriages – as a young lady, a fellow guest, had found the opportunity, in the billiard room after dinner, to murmur in James's ear that Blunt had been the lover of Madeline – and that it was evident, if one should care to glance in a certain direction, that the rabble-rouser and Orientalist had his eye on the daughter next. He could be seen to be making up to Mary Elcho, even as she sits discussing letters burnt or otherwise, with Arthur Balfour.

The maid knocks softly and comes in to remove the ewer and basin, these patterned, like all the other artefacts in the house, with willow leaves and other designs by the great William Morris. Breakfast, she informs the humped, sad-looking gentleman in the single bed piled high with eiderdowns and flossy blankets against the February cold, is at nine in the dining-room. Not for the first time, in his dread of Wilfrid Scawen Blunt and his dislike of the English breakfast as it is invariably presented: kidneys and devilled pheasants' legs, a side of ham like Miss Woolson's stout posterior (so Henry suddenly thinks, and flushes in shame at himself), a dish of kedgeree and rows of boiled eggs awaiting decapitation – not for the first time, the spinner of tales searches his memory for convincing excuses of a more urgent nature than a Sunday evening departure. Illness? – impossible: Mrs Wyndham looks like one of the 'green fruit and God' brigade and the Master might find himself dosed and purged to a degree where his words would fail to issue from him on eventual return to London. A crisis connected with his *oeuvre*? But James can think only of the alarming dip in popularity his books have suffered lately – he had been half hoping *The Aspern Papers*, with its feel of Sherlock Holmes (so he tells himself, at least), will bring in revenue to compensate. But it is not published until September: what emergency could possibly have arisen, which would summon him to town on this cold, dull day?

There is nothing for it but to invent the extreme need of another. Reminded again of Fenimore – the vision of the ham is banished, as James will not go down to breakfast: he will be walking to the post office in East Knoyle instead, to send himself a telegram – he rapidly constructs a call from the near-grave, on the part of his dear friend. Miss Woolson must be suffering – as he knows she does: has she not informed him all too often – from acute neuralgia. Or she has pneumonia – James settles on the latter as he dresses hastily and passes a comb through his hair. There may be difficulty in dissuading his kind and thoughtful hostess from looking up trains to Oxford when he has – of course – no intention of alighting anywhere but Waterloo Station on his journey from Clouds to De Vere Gardens. But he will pull a train schedule from his pocket, and assure Mrs W that he prefers to go by Didcot, as a good practitioner he knows is there and he will take him on to tend Miss Woolson. As the story complicates, begins even to alarm the writer, a gong sounds in the lower regions of the house and the voice of Blunt can be heard directly after, roaring his way along the hall to seize the delicacies on offer. There is just time; and James moves more smartly than he has been used to do of late, in order to leave the house and grounds undetected. Only the ravishing vision of Madeline's daughters, Pamela, Mary and Madeline, as they waft towards the dining-room, leads James to make for the back stairs, and the servants' way out into the rear courtyard at Clouds.

There is no doubt in the Master's mind, as he sits triumphantly in an empty first-class carriage back to London, that his plan has worked wonderfully well. Miss Woolson's proximity to extinction had, perhaps, been overstressed – Pamela, the youngest of the daughters, had burst into tears and gone in search of her pet canaries for comfort after hearing of some of poor Fenimore's sudden symptoms. But, sad though he was to depart from this beautiful house, with its blazing log fires, baskets of fox terriers and lovely young women, James is glad to escape another evening of Blunt and Balfour – and worse possibly, in the form of further loving references to letters past, present and future. That he has taken advantage of Miss Woolson is doubtless true – indeed, James has the impression, on looking back at his own behaviour, of having treated his sad friend as if she is indeed his wife and in urgent need of him. She can certainly never be that: the visit to Clouds, with its evidence of accepted adultery quite unspeakably beyond the code of Miss Woolson – or even, as James must confess, himself – the almost ruthless destruction of the very concept of faithful matrimony, have led him to realise that he and Fenimore would be hopelessly out of their depth in society, as a married couple.

So this tie will not bind him and Constance Fenimore Woolson – so Henry James decides; until, as the train nears the outskirts of London, he remembers the letters they have exchanged, and Fenimore's certain retention of them.

What, after all, will be Miss Woolson's price? – as it was in Venice with Miss Tina – as, horribly, it had been said to be in Florence with Miss Hanghegyi, niece of Claire Clairmont?

The price, as always, was marriage.

# Claire Clairmont's Will

*Florence, 1879*

I Claire Maria Constantia Jane Clairmont spinster now residing at Florence 43 Via Romana and being of sound mind & memory declare this to be my last will and testament.

I elect my dear friend Bartholomew Cini, who for so long a time has enjoyed the esteem of all his friends to be the executor of my will entreating him to undertake this office, feeling well assured that otherwise no respect would be paid to my last will. As a token of my gratitude for all the sympathy which he and his dear departed wife have shown me for more than forty years I bequeath to him the inkstand with which I always write and which is the same with which Shelley the poet wrote many of his poems begging him to have it preserved in his family as an heirloom in memory of one of the most exalted minds that ever breathed.

I further leave to the care of the said B. Cini a tin box containing letters directed by Shelley the poet partly to Godwin the philosopher, partly to me, and a hundred or more letters from Mrs Shelley the poet's wife to me, 36 letters from Trelawny to me, two letters from Sir Percy the poet's son written at the time when he was young, two small and first poetical trials and some doggerel verses by the dowager Lady

Mountcashell Cini's mother in law describing in a humorous manner the qualities of Shelley the poet which made him appear in the eyes of the world as His Satanic Majesty. And in short I leave all my papers to the care of B. Cini and beg him to sell all the letters from Shelley to Godwin or to me, as well as all Shelley's letters or Mrs Shelley's letters to me or others as well as the letters from Trelawny to me and to invest the proceeds in 5 percent Italian national rent in such a manner that only the interest of those stock shall be paid to my niece Paula Clairmont and after her death the whole amount shall go to my dear Georgina Hanghegyi who is living with me. The copies of all letters from Shelley or Mrs Shelley to me I bequeath to my niece Paula begging her to preserve those copies with great care as they would prove of great value in case of the destruction of the originals. All my other papers I leave to Cini that they may be preserved by his family. All my furniture plate linen and books I bequeath to my niece Paula Clairmont begging her to leave them after her death to Georg. Hanghegyi. In a secret shelf of my press will be found 25 bonds of the municipality of Trieste; these I leave to the care of B. Cini and destine them for my niece P.C. The interest amounting to about £15 shall be paid to her every year, but she shall not have any right to touch the capital which is to go after her death to Georg. Hanghegyi. In the savings bank will be found after my death the sum of 1200 lire; these shall pay my funeral expenses which shall on no account exceed this sum. The libretto of the savings bank bearing the number 186 B12 will be found in my strong box. Any amount above the said 1200 lire I leave for the private use of my niece Paula.

I wish to be interred at Antella in a coffin of oak and the following words in English to be inscribed on my tomb:

> In misery she spent her life *expiating* not
> only her faults but also her virtues.

To my dear and beloved Cini I leave the care for my funeral, requesting him or his son John to fulfil or see fulfilled this my last wish, and express to him and his excellent sons my deep gratitude for all their consideration for me.

This is my last will and testament to which I sign my name this the 2nd Day of December 1876 Claire Maria Constantia Jane Clairmont.

My dear friend B. Cini having departed from this life his son John has consented to become the executor of my testament. I name him as such thanking him deeply for his kindness.

July 21st 1877

Claire Maria Constantia Jane Clairmont

# CLAIRE'S LETTERS

Claire Clairmont to Edward John Trelawny
10 Via Barbacane S. Domenico Firenze [*Fiesole*]
6<sup>th</sup> May 1875

My dear Trelawny,

I will endeavour to connect the letters of Shelley
by a short clear narrative. For many reasons I am
afraid it will be a failure; 1<sup>st</sup> my health is so bad, it
is only at intervals of long standing that I can write
even a common letter. Every now and then after a
long repose from all thinking my intellect brightens
up for a day or two, and my ideas take a wide circuit,
and I feel vividly, and I can write a little – then returns
a cloud of dense inactive stupidity over my brain, and
if my life depended on it, in this state, I cannot call up a
thought, or a recollection or a feeling. In what I call my
lucid intervals I generally write to you. However I will
try – notwithstanding the conviction that weighs upon
me that to write even a simple narrative about Shelley,
requires far superior intellectual faculties to any I ever
possessed. On one point I wish to have your opinion:
In all that Mrs Shelley wrote concerning her husband,
there is an ideality, a tender refinement of sentiment
which was worthy of the subject she treated; therefore
it is useless for me to tread in her steps – what

remains for my pen would be trivialities, anecdotes of his private life, and manner of living etc etc – is it desirable to bring these matters before the public – in my opinion it would be much better that they should be buried in silence. He was a wonderful Poet – perhaps in his transcendentalism, greater than any Poet that has ever lived – but when he laid aside his pen and ceased imagining and creating, he became purely and simply a man, generous, tender hearted etc etc – but full of weaknesses that were not in keeping with his great intellect. Do you think I ought to lay this side of the question before the public. Tell me.

Claire Clairmont to Edward John Trelawny
10 Via Barbacane San Domenico Firenze [*Fiesole*]
30th August & 21st September 1875

My dear Trelawny
I am going to make some excuses for not answering your last of 10th July. When you read that word *excuses* you will say as you wrote to me in your letter of last May – 'the unwilling have many excuses – they are always composed of lies' which amused me extremely, and made me wish you were living only a month in my house and then you would know my excuses are Truths. However, now I will only, as regards my not answering yours ere this, say that July and August are two months in which I never do any thing, owing to the great heat which weakens me so much – the only thing I can do is to drink about every half-hour a desertspoonful of wine – else I should die. Now the heat is diminished – and I shall

return by degrees to as much activity as my great age will permit.

You beg me to write to you about Shelley's follies – yet in another letter you say, 'those who have lived in intimacy with a person and disclose their follies are despised by every one'. This was also my own opinion. I read Medwin's Conversations with Lord Byron, and was disgusted with Medwin's baseness, in publishing to the world all the silly speeches, the bad feelings of Lord B – who appears according to Medwin to be what Mr Tighe used to call him, a regular spiteful Old Maid in a country village. Reporting the private life and sayings of a person one has known, is in my opinion only justifiable when it redounds to the credit of the person one reports about; when it can elevate the mind of the reader, and incite him to honourable action – there is a second case in which betraying the secrets of Intimacy is also excusable: that is when the writer is forced to do it, to justify his own reputation, to free himself from calumnies. Lady Byron when she was held up by her husband to the eyes of the whole reading world, as a ridiculous pedantic, ill-tempered, narrow-minded woman, would have been thoroughly justified had she *then* published the tale of cruel wrongs he inflicted on her. But Medwin had no such motive – he did not care how entirely he degraded Lord B – in the minds of all sensible good people, so as he, Medwin (by so doing) could recruit his own poverty-stricken purse. I do not wish therefore to lay before you the follies of Shelley . . .

Now I can write no more – my eyes seem bursting out of my head, (I am) they are so tired. And they become in that state whenever I write more than five minutes at a time.

21st September. I got Browning the Poet through one of my acquaintances to offer the 47 letters I have of Shelley's and the more than a hundred I have of Mary's to Sir Percy, thinking he might like to buy them. But he refused. My niece is overwhelmed with work – she has to make copies of these 147 letters, most of them long – and then to give her lessons to Georgina – this now the cooler weather is come I can now resume – so have more to do than is compatible for my age and strength. I hope you are well – and that you are now in the country enjoying yourself – I would give you an account of the Michel Angiolo fêtes, but we are too poor to go any where, and so saw nothing of them – but I am told they were magnificent. I shall be so glad to hear from you – tho' I dare say you will say I am a story-teller and that I have nothing to do though I say the contrary.

Your Affect. old Friend
Cl. Clairmont

# SILSBEE'S NOTES

Edward Augustus Silsbee's notes on his conversations with Claire Clairmont in the 1870s include: 'Allegra was buried in England, says a story was that she did not die, but a goat's body was substituted and sent there!!' (to Harrow). Trelawny had greeted her notion that Allegra was still alive in a convent with undisguised contempt. On 18 October 1869 he exclaimed: 'You may be well in body; but you have a bee in your bonnet – an insane idea has got into your brain regarding Allegra – Byron certainly wished the child to live and talked of how he should have her educated and marrying her into one of the old Italian family by giving her a good *dota* [*dowry*]'. On 27 November 1869 he continued: 'If I was in Italy I would cure you of your wild fancy concerning Allegra. I would go to the Convent – and select some plausible cranky old dried up hanger on of the Convent about the age your child would now be 52 with & [*a*] story & documents properly drawn up & bring her to you – she should follow you about like a feminine Frankenstein'.

Edward Augustus Silsbee's notes on Claire Clairmont's conversations in the 1870s give some suggestion of what she might have contributed in anecdotes and in acknowledgment of Shelley's human frailties. For example: 'Shelley called Bedrooms "chambers of horrors" they were so jealously guarded – Claire remembered it last night after 50 years – apropos of his bedroom and her own and infer other superstition or ban upon entering them.' She advanced the theory that 'Byron & Shelley after their work on poetry were exhausted & not master of themselves'.

# GEORGINA
## FLORENCE, 1877

The house in Via Romana smells of old men. Even the dreadful rage of Aunt on being informed of the arrival of a 'friend from the past', Signor Gatteschi, didn't stop it being a crowd of three in our already cramped little household: Captain Silsbee, Edward Trelawny and the mysterious Luigi Gatteschi. Silsbee keeps threatening to leave – and so Mama puts on her black felt hat which Aunt says makes her look like a cook – and then Aunt says she is sorry to have spoken this way, she does not wish to side with the elite of this world, as Shelley never did. And when the Massachusetts sea-captain clumps off to the stand in the squashed little hall and takes up his walking stick, poor Mama, hat and all, bursts into a noisy sobbing. There is really no way I can hate her at such times; but I pity her instead, and I know this is a good deal worse, in my heart.

'Sir,' Silsbee is announcing today to Trelawny, who lounges on the one sofa in our sitting-room, sockless as always, contemptuous of manners or what Mama would call 'good behaviour'. He is looking up at Silsbee, giant of a man though he also undoubtedly is, as if he is something Julia's cat Figaro has brought in. 'Sir,' Silsbee says, brandishing the stick while Mama goes for her black felt: she would love to run away too, from this house where she is no more these days than an unpaid housekeeper. '*Mister* Trelawny,' Silsbee goes on, 'you indicated to me a full two days ago that you had information regarding the child Elena Adelaide registered at Naples in the year eighteen hundred and twenty-one as infant daughter of Percy and Mary Shelley, born December twenty-seven in that city –'

'I did not say I had information,' Trelawny roars, very irritated. The annoyance the sea-captain causes him makes the old rebel stand up and walk across the room, as if trying to calm his agitation; but as ever, those vast naked feet, bursting his shoes and mottled blue and red on this stiflingly hot day, seem to have as little idea as their owner of which way he really wants to go. 'If I had the information, I most certainly would not divulge it to you,' Trelawny concludes as he reaches the window. I know he is thinking of Emilia Viviani, whose family live in the palazzo the garden beyond the window belongs to; I know, because Trelawny has often told me of the loves in Shelley's life, and that the poet approved the crazy ideas of Aunt and her friend, then Lady Mountcashell, that the latter would dress as a man, go to the convent where Emilia was shut up, and marry her in order to set her free. 'I believe you have proof that Miss Clairmont was indeed the mother of little Elena Adelaide,' Silsbee insists, coming up behind Trelawny at the window as if the two old fools are engaged in a game of Grandmother's Footsteps. 'On the day of the birth, Mrs Shelley noted Claire's indisposition and a doctor was visited.'

'Miss Clairmont to you,' booms Trelawny, turning suddenly on his heel, so the two grizzled heads are just a centimetre apart, and both men are glowering. 'The fact you lodge here, Captain Silsbee, surely does not put you on an intimate footing with your landlady.'

This last is said with a sneer – only it is a loud sneer, and Mama goes white with fury at the insult to her aunt and, I suppose I must confess, to herself (for if she is not intimate with Mr Silsbee then there is no meaning to the word). Trelawny, knowing he has scored a point, is carried by his wandering feet once more, this time to the fireplace, where he leans against the mantelpiece as if he owned not only Via Romana but Florence too.

'I have documentation,' Silsbee fumes. 'I have lately returned from Naples –'

'And I,' says Mama, which is more pathetic than I have known her for some time. The worst of it is that I can see the horrible Signor Gatteschi is ready to make up to Mama and she will egg him on, in the hope of making Silsbee jealous. The very thought is ridiculous! Silsbee cares only for the relics of PBS – as he so often refers to the dead poet, the shining light in the lives of so many, and of course especially Trelawny. I wonder if the two old rascals will kill each other one day.

'You may have gone to Naples.' Trelawny parrots Silsbee's voice, and it is possible to understand that the imitations he does of Byron and Shelley are very probably as accurate as anyone's could be. Byron he makes smooth and syrupy – and Aunt throws up her hands in hatred at the sound of the wicked man who betrayed her over poor little Allegra. Shelley he does in a child's voice, a tenor that comes right from the back of the throat. But somehow you know that was how he spoke.

'You doubt that I went to Naples?' The offended Silsbee pulls a paper wallet from his pocket and stands there beaming triumphantly.

'I can vouchsafe we went to Naples,' Mama says. But she is tearful again, and the black hat is back on its peg on the stand in the hall. 'We found and spoke with the cheesemonger who was a witness.'

'The birth certificate,' Silsbee continues in a meaningful tone, as if bringing in the humble cheesemonger will clinch the matter. 'And, I may say, a letter from the Neapolitan doctor who attended Claire –'

'Who *said* he attended Aunt at the time,' Mama puts in, like the prize idiot she is.

Trelawny now goes to the door; but he has no sooner flung it open than he bangs it shut again, on seeing Luigi Gatteschi standing there. I wish Aunt would come storming down the stairs as she did when the rogue was announced a couple of days ago, and throw him out for the last time. But she is preparing for – so she thinks – a quiet luncheon with an old friend, Lady Sussex Lennox, who comes with friends visiting Florence who wish to see this relic of the Romantic poets, Lord Byron and Percy Bysshe Shelley. Aunt has said we'll all be thrown in the street – 'even my dear little Georgina' – if Gatteschi is ever seen here again. Yet Mama, who should be instructed by Aunt to rid the house of him, cannot bring herself to let him go. I fear we're all going to find ourselves in the street, for I have never seen Aunt in a rage so horrifying.

'Shelley had loved her for these great storms,' Trelawny told us then, and the way he smiled into his stained beard made me want to run out of the house and escape the faces old men make when they look back on passions long dead and buried now in the box upstairs.

'Shelley had a few scrapes,' Trelawny is now announcing, as if we didn't know already that the gentle poet was far from faithful to his wife Mary, who Trelawny hates and Aunt pretends she loves and has loved all her life long.

'A Scottish beauty who followed Shelley to Italy is the true mother of the child Elena Adelaide,' Trelawny says. 'She is not included in my Records or indeed in my Recollections. She is not of sufficient importance.'

Now we hear Aunt calling down the stairs, wanting to know if the figs and Parma ham are ready prepared for Lady Sussex Lennox. I see Mama flinch, for Julia is not even back from the market yet. Then Trelawny pulls open the door and beams in satisfaction at Gatteschi having vanished into thin air, and Silsbee gives one of his great trumpeting sounds and goes after the old biographer and comrade of the poets as if he will indeed strike him to the ground.

'It is true, Mr Trelawny, that you "saw Shelley plain",' Silsbee thunders as his prey escapes him and makes for the door into the street. 'But I – I have the resources with which to pursue my endless quest for the truth.'

Then the street door in turn bangs, and one old relic at least of the days of Byron and Shelley escapes into the outside world.

I have been up to Aunt's room often enough to bring down a letter from the press by her bed. And I've crept up, while Mama and Mr Silsbee were out in the drawing-room where he likes to spout Shelley's *Queen Mab* and the rest – to return a pilfered document. But I have never had to mount the stairs, as I do now, with a letter: the traffic, as Trelawny might say with one of his dreadful laughs, is all the other way.

The envelope was given to Julia to hand to me by Luigi Gatteschi. Now I know who he is, I am afraid to go up to Aunt. Something about the look of this letter, which has so obviously been opened – years ago – and then stuck down again, makes me know that Aunt will be very cross indeed when she receives it. But my urgent desire to avoid Signor Gatteschi, who had already tried to force cakes and chocolates on me as a reward for delivering this ancient letter, sent me running up as if I was the most willing messenger in the world.

It was Captain Silsbee who'd earlier given us all details of the origins of the paunchy important-looking man who seems to have settled on us here. Gatteschi had known Aunt in Paris years and years ago. 'Maybe he also knows some of her secrets,' Mama said with a smile, her black hat replaced on the stand and all of us agog to hear more. Only Trelawny, I think, was put out by not having heard of Gatteschi: after all, we have been led to believe that Edward Trelawny knows everything there is to be known on the subject of Claire Clairmont, her rapid love affair with Lord Byron; and her more interesting and passionate dalliance with Trelawny himself.

'Your aunt was living in Paris at the time, it is true,' the old rogue conceded, addressing me as if Silsbee simply didn't exist, a trick he'd adopted from the time of his arrival in Via Romana. 'I knew there was trouble, naturally.'

'Miss Clairmont's generosity was outstanding,' Captain Silsbee said in a booming voice. 'Luigi Gatteschi was a very handsome man.'

'And Aunt Claire was smitten by him,' trilled Mama, in a way that made me stare into the fireplace, wishing I could be lifted up there and right out into the sky. 'He is handsome now,' continued poor Mama, clearly hoping to arouse jealousy in the breast of Captain Silsbee.

'No, no,' thundered the Captain, 'the Italian revolutionary was not a lover of Miss Clairmont. It was her stepsister – the inestimable Mrs Shelley – who fell for the charms of the Italian master in Paris. Had Mrs Shelley had the simple sense to wonder how this paragon of beauty –'

'Beauty is a joy forever,' Mama said softly. I honestly wished her out of the house, if not dead just then.

'Had Mrs Shelley considered how our friend Signor Gatteschi could possibly afford to be seen at the opera every night,' Silsbee continued, 'when his sole income was that of a teacher, then poor Claire's sister might have thought again. *And* –' here the Captain wheezed with laughter – 'there were some who preferred not to be taught Italian language by Luigi Gatteschi. He was *too* handsome to be admitted to the household, by fathers and husbands alike.'

Here, Silsbee roared with laughter, and looked over at Trelawny for a similar outburst, as I have noticed one man to another often will.

'Mrs Hanghegyi finds our visitor irresistible even now,' Trelawny said, enjoying the discomfiture of the Captain. 'So you inform us that Mary, Claire's sister – yes, the redoubtable Mary Godwin, the cooler of my dear friend Shelley's warm veins: icy, reserved –'

'Hold on.' Edward Augustus Silsbee, rising from the stool on which he had placed his great form, drew himself to his full height. Edward Trelawny was – as I saw with a sinking heart – obliged to do the same. For a full minute the two men, like beasts from the days before the days not known to Our Lord or his apostles, stood silent in the tiny room. 'No woman, no earthly thing, could deflect the genius which came at his own bidding to the mind and heart of Percy Shelley,' Silsbee said at last.

Some time passed before anyone could understand what crime Signor Gatteschi had committed in Paris. He had, it appeared, been a member of the *carbonari*, the fighters against Austrian occupation of Italy in the 1840s. They were friendly with the charcoal burners of the Northern Italian forests where they hid and fought, and this was why they were called *carbonari*. A failed uprising had driven Gatteschi to abandon his native land and make for Paris. Once there, the only way he could earn money was by giving lessons in Italian. Another member of the *carbonari*, by name Guitera, had accompanied him to that city.

'Much of the correspondence regarding this matter has been destroyed,' said Silsbee, chuckling at his easy triumph over the author of the lives of Shelley and Byron, an author who had arrived declaring himself a celebrity by reason of his knowledge of these legendary people and their wives and mistresses. 'But it is possible to realise that Mrs Shelley made, to put it bluntly, an ass of herself over Gatteschi.'

'Edward!' cried Mama, as I knew she would. Also inevitably, there was a rush to the hat stand and a donning of the black pudding-shaped headgear in full view of all of us. My mother, so it was declared, was leaving the house.

'Luigi Gatteschi had other fish to fry,' intoned Captain Silsbee. 'He had a lusty love affair going with Lady Sussex Lennox –'

'But she comes for luncheon here today,' Mama expostulated.

'Yes yes, they are old friends I daresay by now,' finished Silsbee. 'Forty years have passed after all, my poor little Georgina; Signor G lives near Florence. He must be feeling short of money, as he was all those years ago when one Italian lesson a week had to take him to the opera every night and out to supper afterwards. Mrs Shelley had written him letters – love letters, may I spell it out for you? And he demanded money for their return. Mrs Shelley had nothing in the bank, as the saying goes. And she was forever grateful to her sister Claire, for paying up.'

'The crook, swindler, blackmailer,' Trelawny shouted. Both old men were a dark purple in the face by now.

'Now he returns, and he will have a letter from Mary Shelley's unwise correspondence with him,' Silsbee said.

'I have heard that blackmailers always keep one letter back,' said Mama in a low tone, as if trying to remember lessons learnt in the past. Julia came in; we all stared at her as if she would hold us up to ransom herself – and Trelawny, for whom I now felt truly sorry, hung his head and mumbled. 'Georgina?' Julia shuffled across the floor to me. The smell of Silsbee's interminable pasta Napolitana wafted through from the kitchen – and, in honour of Lady Sussex Lennox, I suppose, there was even a meaty scent thrown in.

'Signor Luigi asked that you take this up to the Signora,' Julia said. She left the room and we could hear her plodding round the under-sized dining-room, laying places for Aunt and her visitor.

Everyone stared at the object Julia had placed in my hand. I cannot remember the order of comments or insistences made by Edward Trelawny and Silsbee, or the cries of dismay from Mama.

But I am holding the letter in my hand and walking up the stairs to Aunt's room. I hear a knock on the door in the hall as I go; and then rapid footsteps as everyone flees the arrival of Lady Sussex Lennox. Aunt will explode with anger, I know; and in my mind's eye I see her carried down the stairs and out of the house, dead as a result of my coming in with a letter.

\*      \*      \*

At first I thought the room I knew so well had been changed overnight – into a hospital, or a dump for old clothes like the rooms Julia and her sister live in, at the end of the frightening road I went down with Allegra on the day I tried to run away. A hospital, because Aunt – as I now see to my horror – is lying in bed with a bandage across her eyes and her arms folded over her chest. She is in her nightdress, and her arms are scrawny and pale, with brown blotches that look as if they're about to grow and grow and take her pale skin away altogether. And the place has the air of a dump because the rags and rubbish strewn on floor and bed are in fact the remains of poor Claire's life and loves, her adventures, sorrows and joys. Shelley has been pulled from the press and exposed as a tattered dream: even the grey shawl, now I come up nearer and stand by the side of the bed, seems on the verge of disintegrating altogether as it lies near Aunt's knees. It is as incapable of giving warmth, perhaps, as the poet had been, in the long life and love Claire and he had shared.

'Is that you, Georgina?' Aunt asks in a weak voice, but I feel a surge of relief as I recognise the fake-invalid tone: Claire has been feeling sorry for herself and has had a tantrum, that is all. Certainly, it is the most violent outburst I've known – the horrid Gatteschi is clearly at the root of it – but Aunt will recover. The letters and papers will go back in the cupboard. And the memories let loose in this room where the curtains have been drawn against the heat of the present, will disappear again into today. 'Do you know there is a Lady Sussex Lennox downstairs who is expecting to eat with you?' I say in as innocent a tone as I can produce. 'Had you forgotten, Aunt? Shall I help you put all this away?'

But Claire Clairmont has known enough liars in her long life, I suppose, to refuse to be taken in by my childish airs. She knows I am afraid to see her there, blindfolded against the comings and goings of a house packed with rogues and scoundrels, all living in the days of freedom and hope she once had loved to describe to me. She will take advantage of me by showing me her unhappiness; and so she does. 'Georgina, have you seen Allegra anywhere?' Aunt says.

A strong smell of pasta Napolitana comes up the stairs and right into the room. Something breadcrumby confirms the probability of veal done *Milanese*, one of Aunt's very favourite dishes. I go to open the bedroom door and a stripe of yellow sunlight comes in.

'Tell Lady Sussex to go away,' Aunt says, back to the feeble voice again. 'I asked you if you'd seen Allegra anywhere. She can help me look for the lost book – wouldn't you say so, Georgina?'

I think, on looking back, that this was the time in my life that I first knew the meaning of guilt, of felony suspected and then caught out; of shame, embarrassment and all those other shadowy sensations known only in a small way to children and then building later, to dominate and dictate behaviour good or bad. I knew, behind my aunt's hooded eyes, lay the straight, honest gaze of the accuser. I knew, as she had lain sleeping or half-awake, that I had been seen and noted all along. I had taken letters and secretly I had returned them; I had removed the most important part of Shelley, his manuscript book, from the bedside table in the little room, where Silsbee liked to flick through it, Mama asleep at his side, but I had not replaced it in Aunt's press. Yet now I know, with this new insight which belongs more to an adult than a child, that this mess of scrumpled papers, old envelopes with seals cracked and now exuding dust, is not the result of a temper fit, as I had thought. It is evidence of a desperate search: at last, Aunt understands herself to be properly stolen from, and is set on the punishing of thief and accomplice both.

'I believe Mr Trelawny sees Allegra,' I blurt out. If anything will distract my aunt from the robberies taking place in her house – and how can they be laid at my door, I was surely obeying Mama, who is so foolishly in love with Captain Silsbee? – it is surely mention of the child.

'Captain Silsbee has left our house,' Aunt intones, clearly seeing my ruse for what it is. She knows perfectly well, of course, that Trelawny never 'sees' Allegra: indeed, his one aim in life is to dissuade Aunt from her conviction that my poor little friend did not actually die at Bagnocavallo all those years ago. The fact I have blundered so hopelessly in my attempt to deflect her, marks me further, so I decide, as a scoundrel as bad as the others in the house. As for the Captain – how can this now deliberately sightless woman have knowledge of his movements, when I left him only minutes ago diving into the room beside the kitchen, to avoid the portly Lady Sussex Lennox? 'He has gone and he has taken Shelley with him,' Aunt says after a long pause, her voice now very grim indeed.

There was literally nothing I could say or do. I tidied, gathered, and collected what remains of Shelley from the corners and hidden crannies where it had been flung or ransacked in the search for the precious book. As I did so, my heart beat faster and my guilt grew by the second. Only at the very end, when I had folded the meagre grey shawl ten times, and replaced it to Aunt's liking by the now primly arranged box in the press, did she remove the blindfold and look at me – tenderly, as I saw, and this made my guilt and agitation all the worse. 'Georgina, you came up here with something for me,' Aunt said.

I should be happy to report that the intuitive powers of my aunt led me to hand over Luigi's letter there and then; but I knew that sunny moods could lead to storms and rampage within a matter of seconds. So I said there was nothing to deliver; and I walked back downstairs with the aged letter crackling hard against my hip, stuffed as it had been in the pocket of my dress. I had to promise Aunt I would return, after I had taken luncheon instead of her, with Lady Sussex and my mother. I would be told, then, what all these papers and letters – Shelley, in short – meant to her, when I came. Aunt would dress, and would take a spoonful of red wine with water, from the chest under the window where she keeps the bottle in case of an attack of her weakness. I would hear of Allegra, too – Aunt might even guide me to her whereabouts now the wicked Edward Trelawny had banished her from her rightful home.

I had heard all this before; and of course I said I would finish the meal as soon as I could and go back there.

I felt no surprise, I must confess, when on arriving downstairs I found the little dining-room deserted, Julia angry, and Mama crying her eyes out in the room tucked away next to the kitchen. Of Lady Sussex there was no sign.

Captain Silsbee had indeed gone – and this time, so it appeared, for good. Shelley's precious manuscript book had gone with him.

I had no desire to return to Aunt's room, after I had shared with poor Mama the overdone meat and the pasta which clung to the side of the bowl as if it would never let go. The shrivelled little *scallopine* looked like dead mens' tongues, wrenched from the heads of all the stupid, lying old men at 43 Via Romana. Mama, who had forgotten this time to remove her hat, looked like a woman at a railway station cafeteria, in transit certainly, but not to anywhere interesting. Filled with the malice Aunt has warned me against so often, I imagined my mother disembarking at a nowhere sort of place out in the Marches beyond Rome – where Trelawny had taken me, I suppose, for other than a visit with Aunt to Lerici I have never been anywhere – and in my mind's eye I saw her walk off into the distance and finally disappear.

'So what are you planning to do this afternoon?' Mama said in a strangled voice as Julia brought in the smart Parma ham and figs – presumably she has begun to feel sorry for Signora Paola, as she always does. It was clear there was no question of another visit from Lady Sussex Lennox, so I helped myself greedily. I grabbed the silky, thin slices of *prosciutto* and crammed them into my mouth.

'Georgina!' my mother sighed, and her eyes became blurred with tears all over again. 'How do you expect to gain a *bella figura* if you stuff yourself like that?'

Mama's Italian, rushed into when we left Hungary, is worse each day. I have an awkward feeling that *bella figura* doesn't mean what she thinks it means; and, despite her sympathy at the Signora's distress (Julia addresses her thus but doesn't fool herself that Mama was ever married, and she knows perfectly well I was born out of wedlock – 'like Allegra,' Aunt says with a trembling smile), I think I hear a chuckle from the kitchen. The most embarrassing example of Mama getting Italian wrong was when she fondly addressed Julia's little niece as *'stupidina'*: plates were thrown in the kitchen, and then Julia and all her visiting relatives marched out of the house and were gone for the rest of the day.

Why do I remember all this? Because, I suppose, the absence of Edward Silsbee is more potent than I could have expected it to be. The months before he came, when only Mama and Aunt and I were here, return like a memory of halcyon days. And absence makes you think of presence – of what I couldn't help myself from seeing in the little room off the kitchen, the room he paid Aunt a steep price to rent, as everyone knows, so he could get his hands on her papers when she died. But he didn't bother to wait: he's gone anyway, taking Aunt's most treasured possession, as somehow she knew he had; and without a word to anyone, including, as it must seem, Mama. He'd proposed marriage to her, once: I'd had the misfortune to hear him when I sat studying a book of Latin verbs Aunt had given me, at the table in the dining-room where we had our unsatisfactory luncheon today. 'Cara Paola,' Silsbee said. I hated it when the old American pretended to be a Florentine. 'Cara, shall we get married, do you think? Will you give me your answer soon?'

Those days seem long ago, now. Mama collapsed straight after the meal and went to cry on the rumpled, smelly bed in the little room. Will Aunt try to find another lodger? She'll never get the rent Captain Silsbee paid, I heard Julia say.

The afternoon drags on, too hot to go out into and too airless to sleep in, perhaps its only use is for crying, like Mama, or for letting loose memories of the lost past, like Aunt upstairs in her room. The Italians, of course, know how to deal with this terrible, baking heat: those who can't afford to go up into the hills make islands of darkness and cool, with drawn blinds and a breeze caught now and then through a long window shaded but open – or a balcony where basil grows, lending calm and a refreshing air to the room. We, who do not know how to arrange ourselves in these ferocious Florence summers, must wait for evening as best we can.

But today I find myself unable to bring Aunt the happiness – which means, always, the audience – she

122

so badly needs. I cannot listen to the memories, fixed by now it seems, yet changing like the sea she took me to visit, at Lerici.

I saw nothing of interest in the house where Aunt had lived at the time, with her stepsister Mary and the young woman Jane who liked to play the guitar and sing.

I have no wish to inherit the secrets Aunt forgets each time she has confided them. I know all about the tragedies at Casa Magni now, the white house we visited together on the sea-front at Lerici. But they mean nothing at all to me.

I am sitting, mooning over the glass of water Julia has clouded with red wine – Mama doesn't like the habit of feeding wine to children but Aunt's habit of a spoonful on the hour, mixed with water, has somehow caught on – when the front door opens and then the door of the dining-room, with Trelawny's head poking round it. Not for the first time, I think of how the old rascal, with his tales of Greek caves and of the daggers he keeps still with their ancient bloodstains in his house in London – does actually bring his memories into the here and now. I can see the past, when he describes it; I can even cry or laugh. The fact these recollections are very probably blown up out of all recognition, doesn't seem to matter a bit.

'So how was the luncheon?' Trelawny asks when I have followed him into the *salone*. 'Did Claire behave herself, little Georgina?' Trelawny has flung himself onto the painted wood and cane sofa which Aunt must have found in Russia, for it has bouquets of roses and cherubs on it. 'A meeting after all these years with Lady Sussex! – Did they discuss the bribe your good-hearted relative had to pay to the Prefecture of Police by way of her friend Mr Knox, to assure a raid on Signor Gatteschi's house and the securing of the letters? I wouldn't have missed the conversation for the world – but, as it happens, I had another engagement.'

As he spoke Trelawny looked at me with a distinctly challenging air. It had never been known for him to change either the way he talked or his clothing for the sake of an invitation, and he frequently boasted that the only engagement he recognised was a battle concerning a matter of life or death.

I explained that the luncheon had failed entirely to materialise. 'Captain Silsbee has gone,' I ended my account of the sad meal where my mother wept, and Lady Sussex, departing just before I came down and leaving what I had been brought up to believe was the odour of sanctity behind her – that is, a pungent smell of violets – had not even met my aunt. 'Violets,' mumbled Trelawny, and the mist settled in his eyes that was a sign of his return to those times he shared with Claire and Mary, the two women, as he so often told me, whom he had truly loved – then, in Mary's case, came to hate. 'Lady Sussex can have no odour of sanctity.' And he roared with laughter at the notion. 'But the thought of violets moves me, Georgina, for they grow on Shelley's grave – in the Protestant cemetery in Rome, you know. Violets – they belong to Shelley . . . and even, though he would resist the idea of the existence of a deity, to God. Now, as you tell me, they are to be associated also with women of loose morals, such as Lady Sussex Lennox.'

'Captain Silsbee took the manuscript book,' I said. 'I believe Aunt must have seen him leave, from her window, with his bags, and she understood she had been robbed. Poor Aunt,' I added, but from a mistaken sense of piety, I fear, and not because I was sorry for the old lady. Why, after all, had Aunt not succeeded in obtaining a good price for the papers she had told us again and again were of inestimable value? How had she permitted so blatant a theft, the removal from the house of her greatest treasure, to take place? 'I'll wager Paula gave marriage as the price, when that scoundrel Silsbee said he'd stay if he could get his hands on the papers at the time of Claire's death,' Trelawny said grimly. I noted that the storm of anger I had expected, on giving the news of the old sea-captain absconding with the best part of Shelley, had not come about. Perhaps, I surmised, Trelawny placed more value on the ashes, the jawbone and the heart of his hero (this latter, frustratingly, enshrined in England, the property of young Percy and his wife), than he did on the poet's record of his struggle with words. His own *Recollections* were, it occurred to me, more important in the eyes of Trelawny than the real thing, as penned in a manuscript book by Percy Bysshe Shelley. 'Claire was a fool not to have kept the papers under lock and key' was all Trelawny said after a contemplative silence. 'Silsbee was continually going up there, she told him a pack of lies and he believed the lot.' And here Trelawny let out a roar of laughter.

Trying to explain to the old man the subtleties of the friendship between Claire and Silsbee, in which I played a role as go-between, carrier of letters and returner of semi-stolen papers 'borrowed for research', was obviously impossible. I had let Aunt down; she had been robbed of the important manuscript book; while her spoken memories the irresponsible Silsbee took elsewhere, to transcribe and sell. 'Well, Georgina,' says Trelawny, in a new, businesslike voice, 'you haven't told me yet what you did with the document entrusted to you by our friend Luigi Gatteschi. He will be back shortly, I have no doubt, to collect his ransom money. An old affection for Jane Clairmont – Jane as she was known when young – leads me to hope he didn't extract too much of a fortune from her.'

'Certainly not,' I reply, and found myself flushing at the thought that the old mountebank – as Silsbee had had the impertinence to name him – could accuse me of being a part of a blackmailing of my aunt. 'I have it here,' I go on, still very red in the face.

'In your pinafore?' says Trelawny, laughing but then looking very serious as I pull out the incriminating letter from the top of the frilly drawers Julia complains at having to iron, because Mama has other things to keep her busy. 'I'd say you were a little minx if I didn't know better.'

I hand over the letter and it feels to me as if a weight has been lifted from my person of which I had no notion. Even when Trelawny, whom I had almost come to trust and like, grabbed my arm and lifted me right up on my toes to kiss me – I went on feeling huge relief at having rid myself at last of this terrible letter. Trelawny, as uninterested all of a sudden in squeezing and dribbling over me with his great beard and moustaches as he had been keen to molest me a moment earlier, now transfered his attention to the missive in its ancient, stained envelope, and I was dropped, quite literally, on the hard floor of the drawing-room. 'Hmm,' says the old man as he scans the envelope, 'there is little way of mistaking Mrs Shelley's writing – or of finding oneself pleasantly surprised by the contents, either.'

By the time the letter has been read over twice by the old man, I find another feeling succeeds that of ecstasy at being relieved of it. What if Gatteschi comes in now, admitted by Julia (who favours him: is he not Italian?)? Suppose he finds me here with Trelawny – who reads the letter and gives his loud laugh, though there is a measure of annoyance in it now? 'Mary had, alas, a commonplace mind,' Trelawny pronounces as I make my way to the window overlooking Via Romana. (I had seen Luigi hovering across the street before; on being espied from the window opposite he usually crossed the road and pretended to wander aimlessly in the Boboli Gardens until the coast was clear.) 'The goose Mary was in love with this petty crook and swindler,' Trelawny says in a magisterial tone, but there is regret mixed with his satisfaction. 'Of the two, it was Claire – dear Jane – I loved,' he goes on, as if this could have any bearing on the matter in hand.

I return from the window, glad to have seen no sign of Gatteschi – though Mama's black hat, as I note with alarm, lies trampled in the gutter. Has she lost all control of her emotions? – has she thrown it out there to be picked up by a beggar? The street is empty, except for a nun who stands a few doors down, her eyes trained upwards, as if in prayer. From time to time, as I note with surprise, the veiled head turns towards us: is this an omen, as I now begin to think, of bad and then worse days to come?

'My dear little Georgina,' Trelawny says in a soft voice I have learned to mistrust, 'tell me what you think we should do with this letter. I value your opinion, you see, my dear. Did I ever confide in you the great love affair which overcame me during the writing of the *Recollections*? How I took a young mistress when I lived in Wales near the river Usk, and swept her from her carriage to carry her up Llanbadoc Rock before installing her in my house? Oh, much to the irritation of my wife, as well as the respectable people of Usk, I can assure you! Samson and Delilah – you know of them, Georgina, I imagine, despite the scanty education you suffer as a result of your aunt asking a very great deal too much for her papers, and my being therefore quite unable to sell them.'

As Trelawny spoke, he went to the mantelpiece, looked down into the empty grate and chuckled loudly. 'Claire would in all probability pay over the odds to suppress this sad cry of thwarted passion from Mary to Gatteschi,' now comes from him, in a thoughtful tone that has me turning and going to the door. However distressed Mama may be, she is at least grown-up – she brought me here – why should I remain alone with a man now subsumed with mischievous glee? What will he do with me, when he has disposed of the letter as he has clearly chosen to do?

I run; but Trelawny's left hand comes out to catch me as I go, a huge paw adorned with the 'magic' rings he has explained to me when I was no more than a child in his eyes – elephant's hair, one of them (but I forget which charm it can supposedly perform) and turquoise he says comes from the distant mountains of Tibet. I am bound to Trelawny's side; and so I watch the letter as it burns there in the grate.

'Your aunt's motives would be good,' Trelawny says, 'in paying the detestable Gatteschi. She fears any stain on the memory of Shelley may reach his son, the dull and blameless Sir Percy, who lives with the shrine of his father amongst the English fields. She protects Shelley all these years – though she dislikes as much as I do the religion Lady Shelley has endowed her husband's late father with, after death. Claire will suffer, little Georgina, for Shelley if she has to.'

The letter burns slowly at first and gives off a blue flame I suppose must come from the sealing-wax – though it's easier to believe the devil dances in that fire, invited there to spite the blackmailing Gatteschi when he comes to find the gold he believes I've got for him. 'Cold, pious . . . who could have thought Mary had those words and thoughts in her?' Trelawny mutters, as the last fragments of burnt paper go up the chimney. He sounds, I confess, not entirely delighted with this discovery of the passionate nature of Mrs Shelley.

A bang on the front door leads Trelawny to let me

go suddenly, so I stagger on the way out of the room. Luigi it must be – and Luigi must – somehow – be prevented from coming into the *salone* with its smell of sulphur and the fragments of the letter Claire's sister wrote to him, floating out from the fireplace. How, without Mama's help, can I deflect him? And for a mad moment I pray that the overtures my mother made to the Italian, when trying so foolishly to arouse jealousy in the breast of the departed Silsbee, may have resulted in a corresponding interest on Gatteschi's part.

'Georgina!' Trelawny's reach is long and there is no way of evading it. I am wrenching open the door of the room when a presence announces itself outside in the narrow hall. 'Stop!' I beseech the old man as he struggles to bring me up close to him again – 'Gatteschi is here, turn him away.'

But Trelawny, as I see to my utter dismay and incredulity, has dropped to his knees in the middle of the small drawing-room. His arms are outstretched, his eyes wild and his voice choked with emotion. 'Marry me, Georgina!' he implores as the door slowly opens and I see – I recognise – the nun who had been standing in Via Romana as she pauses there. 'Your aunt will have no need for you, my dear Georgina – for, look, I have restored her daughter Allegra to her! A veritable Frankenstein! Come to London with me, Georgina – you won't be worried by my Welsh bride; she remains in Usk.'

I stand for what seems like a year between the two people now occupying the room where my aunt likes to entertain the Florentines with her stories of the

Romantic poets and the past. To one side kneels
Edward Trelawny, a supplicant who looks as if he
is carved in stone and left to weather in the English
rain, so battered and indistinct have his features now
become – and on the far side, blocking my escape
to Mama's room and to the outside world – the
middle-aged woman Trelawny says is Aunt's Allegra.

I tremble at the trick the horrible old man has
played on poor Aunt. For the nun I recognise from
the convent at Bagnocavallo, and I know she is not
Allegra. Trelawny was with the Mother Superior in
the chapel there and I saw the gold coin as it slipped
from his hand to hers.

'Allegra will care for her mother,' Trelawny declaims,
still on his knees in the centre of the room. 'Marry
me, Georgina!'

# HENRY AND CONSTANCE
## LAKE GENEVA, OCTOBER 1888

Constance Fenimore Woolson and Henry James, divided
as so often – and in this case by a stretch of water, blue
with the 'gush and rush' of the Rhône (Henry James:
from Constance there is no description of Lake Geneva,
either placid or stormy) – will nevertheless meet today
for luncheon, a late meal to be taken after Henry's
own rush across Europe from a London grown stale
and dingy with long occupation. His gush, Constance
expects, will contain news of the prodigious output of
the Master since they last exchanged confidences.
Stories, tales, novellas; and now, embarked on a theatrical enterprise, *The Tragic Muse*, Henry has come here,
as he has made clear in letters to several friends, to work,
and not simply for the 'velvet' of the Alps as they hang
over the Lake, or for any other description-prompting
vision. One or two (his brother William, chiefly) are
apprised of the fact that Miss Woolson and James ply
their pens at a mile's distance from each other, on the
shores of the lake. A perfect arrangement, Henry is
inclined to stress: nothing could be easier than for the
two dear and intimate friends to visit each other when
they please, over water.

Constance fills in the morning before the arrival of
Henry by going to revisit Coppet, the grand house

on the lake where Madame de Staël, creator of the world-famous *Corinne*, had lived. Constance herself has written a story, 'At the Château of Corinne', in which a gifted woman writer, falling in love with a learned and celebrated man, discovers she must suppress her creativity entirely if she wishes to become his wife. The story of Corinne, the female genius who dies of love, has drawn her for years: indeed, her own story was written seven years ago. It is only now, since reading the tribute, so loving and so full of hidden daggers, that James has published in *Harper's* on the subject of his best-selling friend Constance Fenimore Woolson, that she has permitted her story to be printed. His 'Fenimore' has shown Henry, who must surely have read 'At the Château of Corinne', her knowledge of his demand for sovereignty: she has been shown to ask something of him, while he had considered himself at last to be enjoying a disinterested friendship with a woman. Constance has demonstrated, with her story of the living death suffered by a woman who dares to write – or succeed with her writing – when associated with a genius such as James, that she understands the price she would need to pay. Yet – more galling and humiliating still than the contemplation of a life behind a veil of silence, is the strong possibility that this sacrifice will not after all be asked of her. The Master comes to Switzerland to write. There will be no proposal of marriage after all.

Coppet is dark in its little wood by the banks of Lake Geneva. Already, as Constance makes her way up the steps and into the *salon* where the portrait of her heroine hangs – Madame de Staël in a yellow turban, ugly and fascinating under the Oriental headgear, a female pasha where Constance, in her desire to assert herself, has so dismally failed – there comes an intuitive knowing that the man she quite simply loves and devotes her thoughts to, will turn away from her once more. Madame de Staël seems to smile, as Constance wanders disconsolately around the room, finally settling on a long seat covered in an elaborately patterned eau-de-nil brocade, just below the dominatrix in the picture. Germaine de Staël, daughter of Louis XVI's finance minister, M. Necker, bursting with self-confidence and riches such as a little Miss Woolson from the New World could never equal, would have proved an excellent match for Henry – indeed, as the small, almost deaf woman dwarfed by the great room seems to say silently to the dead woman above her on the wall, she, Germaine, would most likely, in that clash of titans, have won.

It is blue and gold out on the lake, and Constance is drawn there by the sheer weight of her depression and an increasing longing for an end to this life of moving, baskets and all, from Florence to Oxford, to Cairo and Corfu. Now, as she finds herself in the middle years which so favour men but which, in the case of Miss Woolson at least, appear solely to render her invisible, she needs to settle in one place: she needs not to be lonely any more; she dreams of De Vere Gardens and of a house in the country, somewhere in England. But the dream peters out each time, usually in an expanse of water such as this one: bland, blueish, rippling with memory and the pointlessness of years to come. Constance, after walking politely in the group of over-tended trees at the verge of Coppet land, stares down in the direction of the old town of Geneva, where Jean-Jacques Rousseau wrote of freedom and Calvin taught predestination. She no longer knows which she believes in, for the improving of the soul, for Madame de Staël enjoyed the liberty of privilege, and she, Constance, is chained to her creed of privacy, reticence, deference to those she perceives as greater than herself. Have her life, and all her writing successes, been in vain? She could never die of passion, as Corinne had done; but – and she stoops to pick a pebble and throws it with a sudden fury into water black now with the gathering of storm clouds overhead – she can refuse, if Henry refuses her unspoken wish, to grant him the possession of her when she dies.

Yet there is no denying that the first sighting of the man she loves restores Constance, as so often before, to a different knowledge, that of hope and of a desire to live. The waiting boat which takes her to the lakeside restaurant where they will eat, succeeds only by a second or two in depositing her there safe and dry. Thunder makes itself heard, as the old friends greet each other under the canopy, at a table carefully selected for its fine view of Alps and lake. If their reflection heaves and disintegrates in water dark and hissing with the ferocity of the rain, Constance Fenimore Woolson and Henry James appear unaffected by the upheaval all around them. They order *filets de perche*; they open out their napkins like fans in a courtship dance; and they both burst into speech at once.

How could Fenimore have gone so long without the lift of spirits and the sheer, if sometimes malicious, enjoyment involved in talking about 'the business' with the writer most attuned to the subtleties of exposing the corrupt, forlorn or conniving heroes and heroines who come to life under his guiding hand? Doesn't she feel herself uplifted, complimented on her looks one minute (she forgets 'Miss Woolson' at these times: she knows James is contrite at the poisoned praise hc has lavished on his greatest woman friend in his article for *Harper's*) and the next, better still, she finds herself deferred to, an expert on the ways and means of approaching a subject never before offering itself for extrapolation. She had forgotten, so she tells herself, the sublime intelligence and charm of the man, in his forties and with grey showing at the edge of his beard, head bald and gleaming in the rays of a watery sun now succeeding the frenzy of the storm; she had failed, as ever, to retain a clear picture of the essence – if such a thing were possible – of Henry James. He makes of her two women, she decides: the human being, giver of herself to others, willing performer of every sacrifice a friend or supplicant might need; and the writer, one who understands the currents in the intercourse between men and women and has no fear in exposing weakness and cowardice in her characters, belabouring the women, even, for their very ability to do as she does, and sacrifice their lives on the altar of duty. James knows, as his friend Robert Louis Stevenson knows, the extent to which a writer can weave between good and evil, in his desire to paint the temptations of the world – and briefly, as the perch arrives and the waiter pours a fine white wine from the Jura into their goblets, Fenimore enjoys the heady sensation, as her companion's large grey eyes rest solemnly on her, of being both Dr Jekyll and Mr Hyde. The air Calvin breathed comes down onto the lake, and even if she knows that women are not taken seriously as writers by her mentor, Henry, she begins to believe she sees in his wondering gaze an acceptance of her superiority to other scribblers of her sex. She has been appointed, even, to kill with the accuracy of her aim: writer as Justified Sinner in the eyes of God. Foolish Fenimore! She is neither better nor worse than any of the other failed artists born into women's bodies: no amount of effort will rectify her own original sin, that of being born a woman.

Henry now talks of death. At least it's a subject close to Fenimore's heart; and, recovering from her brief burst of pride, the ever-constant Miss Woolson adds melodiously to her fellow luncheon-eater's symphony of regret on the subject of Lizzie Boott, a young friend and new mother, lately a dweller at Bellosguardo and thus a neighbour of the villa Constance likes to think of as her own, I Brichieri. It is appalling, hums Fenimore, afflicted by the latest 'drums' inserted in her ears to facilitate her increasingly problematic hearing. 'And no two men could make a stranger combination than the father and husband she leaves behind: a bohemian and a gentleman.'

As soon as she has spoken, it is obvious that platitudes issue from the mouth of the lady fortunate enough to find herself seated opposite Henry James. A host of *idées reçues*, in the bored silence which follows Constance's words, now fill her mind – and worse than this, it is obvious that the Master senses the presence of these oft-repeated banalities. 'How do you find the perch?' he enquires, as the backbone is lifted tenderly from the grey and pink flesh. 'So, so sad,' Miss Woolson cannot prevent herself from blurting, all excitement at being the possessor of a dual nature quite disappeared. She is Constance Woolson now, no more, just the grand-niece of the famous James Fenimore Cooper. 'Yes,' James concurs – for now he has in the last minute gone from Lizzie Boott to the subject of his ailing sister, Alice. 'Still at Leamington, how she can endure the curates and the company of Dr Baldwin alone I cannot imagine.'

Constance purses her lips, in order to disguise a small fishbone lodged in the upper jaw. 'It is so sad,' she repeats, indistinctly enough for Henry's look to glaze: has Fenimore developed a penchant for too much wine? Is she – an impossible suggestion – about to become quite drunk?

'She was grateful for your invitation to Florence,' Henry goes on, in the manner of one stranger talking to another in a railway carriage. 'You offered her the balmy air of Bellosguardo – but her health would not permit the travelling.'

When Constance has said she regrets very much that Henry's invalid sister had been unable earlier in the year to visit her at I Brichieri – and after a series of manoeuvres with the large white napkin to remove the fishbone (these regarded by Henry with extreme distaste, his attempts to look away rewarded by an admiring stare from an adjacent table containing a young man with the look of a James acolyte: he can possibly be spoken to, later) – there is no doubt that the luncheon, so sparkling at the start and now so stodgy and disappointing, will do best if consigned to the category of awkward first meetings after a long absence. Constance has plenty of these; she is as liable to forget the awful silences and lack of interest in her – either as sacrificing woman or as writer – which Henry can produce, as she is capable of delighted surprise at the encouragement and affection – there is no other word for it – which he can show his 'Fenimore'. Now, as so often before, she has said the wrong, unacceptable thing. Summing up the male relatives of the cherished Lizzie Boott in that way! – why, she could have been as crass as the lowest biographer.

'Fenimore, I have this to give to you,' James says when a sorbet of an exquisite paleness has been placed before them. And he pulls two volumes from a small case – the case where he keeps his most private papers and jottings, of stories and novels in progress.

'Henry . . .' murmurs Constance. The spoon bearing the *poire* sorbet lingers just under her nose, and she sees herself as almost pretty, a portrait of a *jeune fille* with her neat features and sweet expression, about to receive a gift from the Master himself. She glances, aware of the fantasy she entertains but radiant once more nonetheless, at the young man at the next table as he gazes at poor dear Henry. There is little doubt about it, the great writer is known everywhere; and although he had explained his reason for choosing Switzerland rather than France or Italy as the destination for his 'working holiday' (Constance hoping for something more) as a country where he could pass incognito, he had clearly been quite wrong. The light of proximity to celebrity is not unwelcome, however, for Constance at least: here she is, about to be presented with a gift by Henry James! She poses deliberately, under the stare of the interested young man.

'*The Aspern Papers*,' James says, neither with modesty nor with pride. The thought he is concealing some painful feeling flits across Constance's mind and then goes away again.

Henry James leans across the table; he is trying, so it appears, to muster some of the fine early mood which had captured them both on meeting – and there is a stagey sound to his voice. (Though, as Constance admits to herself later, the 'drums' in her ears could be responsible for leading her to hear this.)

'Alas I must return to my work,' James says hastily, as Constance, still evincing the naïve delight with which authors expect the gift of one of their books to be greeted, riffles through the endpapers and finds his inscription to herself.

'Oh, Henry, I cannot thank you enough,' Constance begins, as the James-worshipper rises to his feet and makes his way over to the table. 'I shall so much enjoy reading . . .'

Henry gives an order for a carriage to take him to the Hôtel de L'Ecu. He pays; and as Constance burbles (thus she revisits the scene of her humiliation, so often enacted before, of herself making female noises while Henry sustains a disapproving silence) the great man turns once on his way from the dining-room, to gaze at the young man, arrested in mid genuflection by the side of the table.

Then Henry goes. His gaze has been long and piercing; and none of it has been expended on Miss

Woolson. She must make her way back to her own hotel now, in the boat earlier requested for her by the management.

Lights go out around Lake Geneva early, in these out-of-season weeks, and by ten o' clock there remains only one lit window in the modest little *pension* where Miss Woolson has decided to put up, baskets, valises and all (the 'all', as Henry is uncomfortably aware, consists of the battered old trunk where Constance's correspondence is stowed: at least, he is able to reassure himself over a last *eau-de-vie* with Nicolas, the charming young Swiss who introduced himself after Mr James's companion had left the restaurant, there can be no reason to expect a letter from poor Fenimore while they are lodged so close together in the vicinity: the trunk need not be opened; there is no danger of a prying scoundrel coming near the trove).

Lights go out; but the lamp in the first-floor room in the *pension* run by Madame Lutèce burns on. A crowd of night insects – moths, daddy longlegs and the occasional foolhardy mosquito – is assembled at the window, which Constance leaves ajar. She needs air; she may stifle or suffocate at any minute: she must read and reread until her eyes are dim and the dancing, fluttering visitors take control of the domain. For Constance Woolson has been made ill with alarm and horror. She has been confronted, in this low-eaved room where the sole mirror hides discreetly behind the door of a ponderous black walnut cupboard, this concealing her image, magnified, as she imagined it, a thousand times. In the two-volume set of his new work just published a month back, *The Aspern Papers*, her dear friend Henry – her 'intimate' friend indeed – has travestied her for all time and for all the world to see. In this tale of papers prized above love or even friendship, the gifted author has shown his Fenimore as – in his words (and these she can barely see now, as the inclement weather of earlier in the day begins its slow return and a miasma appears to fill the room, a rain cloud entering the soul and body, blinding the eyes and choking the throat) – a 'ridiculous and pathetic old woman'. She, Constance Fenimore Woolson, 'deluded and infatuated' with the scholarly narrator, is shown as a goose.

A wind gets up, and waves, polite at first and then aggressive in their determination, can be heard slapping against the little wooden jetty where Constance had been deposited after luncheon. She had been mortified then – had she really been so vulgar as to utter the pronouncement on the relics of Lizzie Boott that she had heard so many times, from women lacking in distinction, and without the 'fine ear' for which Henry has often appraised her? Had she simply been nervous, knowing as she knew he did also, that this is the time when they may make the decision – when *he* could conceivably decide, despite his sister's illness in England and the prospect of a curtailment of his social life, to propose marriage to the most important woman in his life? If she had not come out with that trite judgement, might she, at this moment, be celebrating – a word too difficult to place in reality, she cringes from it and substitutes 'acknowledging' – an engagement between herself and Henry James?

But this is impossible to contemplate. The cosy, slightly pompous dining-room at the Hôtel de L'Ecu, empty save for a radiant middle-aged couple, the lady (well, why not?) sporting a diamond solitaire on the fourth finger of her left hand and the gentleman, announcing this had been his mother's engagement ring, fade from view and Constance is left alone again. She lifts her ringless hand to the flickering oil lamp; and, driven by the mounting insinuations of the bad weather outside, the mosquito flies in, drones so the drums in her ears buzz in concordance, and bites her just below the wrist.

The pain is as sudden as the stab Constance remembers, all those years ago, when, creeping into her grandfather's study, she had taken a paper knife to forbidden pages and inflicted a shallow but never-to-be-forgotten injury on herself. She sobs, suddenly and violently, and then leaps to her feet as if come on by a just-noticed foe. The first volume of *The Aspern Papers* is picked up and hurled at the insect, as it weaves its way towards the narrow bed, coverlet turned down for the night, which awaits its occupant with the certainty of the grave. The book misses; the mosquito goes unheedingly on. And now, the fury and determination in Miss Woolson (that fury and determination which has driven her to write and write, until she falls exhausted at the tenth draft and succumbs to the inevitable depression) lead her to seize the second volume and throw it wildly at the wall. This is the volume where the dim Miss Tina, niece of the cunning old lady upstairs in the Venetian palazzo concocted by Henry James, is shown as a helpless supplicant for the love and hand of the man who cannot, even for the sake of the priceless papers, imagine himself as her husband. 'It won't do . . . it won't do . . .' the words of James's horrified thief and poem-reciter come echoing from the primly bound book, then resonate across the water from the Hôtel de L'Ecu. Oh, it would never do, to find oneself actually having to marry Miss Constance Woolson!

The book hits the mosquito fair and square and carries its booty with it, to the whitewashed wall behind the bed. Here, the insect splatters and finally falls, leaving a trail of brownish blood. Constance's blood, a mark she will not try to remove, turns quickly to an autograph, a smear.

The light burns on, until the oil is gone, and the obscured moon throws in an occasional brightness, soon swallowed up again by cloud.

Had Henry 'led her on'? Had he taken advantage of the devoted Fenimore, all these years, only to humiliate her in public by making eyes – yes, she will shout the words out loud, if she wishes to – at a German youth today? Did he, even, do this purposely, at the time of presenting Miss Tina, the 'younger' Miss Bordereau (as Constance knows herself to be, and described as 'of minor antiquity' besides) with the infinitely cruel description of herself contained in *The Aspern Papers*? Is the man truly a publishing scoundrel, exposed by his own novella on the subject of greed for a poet's papers?

It is intolerable, to stay cooped up in this small room with the waves on the lake now crashing below and the darkness humming with further winged insects –

all, as Constance in her terror and rage, believes – out for her blood.

Without taking a shawl or coat, and shod only in the thin slippers in which she had earlier supped frugally in the *pension*, Constance flies down the stairs of the small house, fiddles with the key in the lock of the French windows onto the pier outside, and releases herself into the storm. She had not failed to take note of the fact that the door of the walnut cupboard in her room had swung open, as if in subjugation to the dark forces outside; and Miss Woolson's last vision, before escaping into the gale, was of herself: dumpy, distraught and forever undesirable.

Henry James bids farewell to his new acolytes – there are several by now, ardent admirers of the Master, and seemingly whipped up from thin air by young Nicolas. All are eager to discuss James's work and to mention, modestly of course after a time, that they too are here to 'ply their pens' – just as Henry had described himself and Constance to his brother William, very much as if he and the devoted Fenimore were already married, and choosing to live separated by a stretch of water now grown once again unpleasantly choppy. 'Miss Woolson?' asks one of the band; for Nicolas has spread the news of the female companion, and of the froideur which had descended suddenly – and, apparently unexpectedly for both of them – on the table under the canopy earlier that day. 'Miss Woolson is a writer, I believe?'

'Indeed Miss Woolson is a writer,' James replies impassively. He cannot decide yet how the works of his dear friend should best be portrayed. 'If you care to, you may find my portrait of Miss Woolson in a recent issue of *Harper's*. I believe a fair picture is given there, of her achievements.'

'But is she a *good* writer?' the friend of Nicolas insists. James, flattered at the attention he has lately received, narrows his eyes and examines the student – for such he must be – before concluding his inquisitor must have Teutonic origins. However, what is wrong with that? They are adamant; they do press one so; but is this not the moment to establish for once and for all who Miss Constance Fenimore Woolson may actually be? A German will always prise the truth out of one, in the end. 'Miss Woolson is a good friend,' James says. He picks up a pencil from the rattan table just cleared of coffee cups and cognac glasses by the sleepy waiter and holds it suggestively aloft: for a second, the apostles wonder if their leader has decided to go so far as to write something, a tale perhaps, there and then.

'But is she a good writer?' presses the young man who has now owned to the name of Hildebrand. 'Do you admire her, sir?'

Henry makes to rise, and the group, gazing with some irritation at young Hildebrand as the cause of this undesired departure, close in round the great man, so he subsides once more into the cushions of the deep armchair from which he has pontificated and demonstrated his capacity for long silences, alternately. 'It is possible to find qualities which lead to the strongest bonds of friendship, in a person,' James says finally, as Nicolas, bearing a glass of water, places it before the Master on the low table. 'It is also possible, if that person is a writer, to say one has no sense of their value, as a writer, to the world in general. In short –'

'But how is it possible to feel an affection for someone – for a writer,' cries the impassioned young man, 'and to dislike what they write? Surely, the man –' and remembering, he checks himself as if already defeated and goes on – 'or woman, who writes, gives of themselves to the work they produce? How can you like the human being and not the book?'

'Ah.' James shakes his head; and this time, as he rises more steadily, the little band of worshippers make way for him to go towards the large screen by the ornamental doors and thence up the staircase to the principal suite, long ago booked by his aide in London, at the Hôtel de L'Ecu. Henry is tired; very tired. It is obvious the students have no real understanding of his art, of the sacrifices necessary to its perfection, of the decision he has just made all over again to remain a bachelor for the rest of his life. 'It won't do,' he murmurs, as he rounds the velvet-embossed screen, 'it won't do.'

The disappearance of Henry James is succeeded by a burst of talk from Nicolas and his friends, some protesting, like Hildebrand, that there can be no true friendship between people who dislike each other's work – or, if in the case of the celebrated author and the middle-aged woman of modest appeal with whom he had been seated at luncheon, it was a case of reverence on one side, and a barely suppressed contempt on the other, then a strange kind of friendship must exist, albeit a common one between writers, particularly male and female. The difficulties inherent in such relationships drive the students, who are now escorted from the

Hôtel de L'Ecu by the manager with some acerbity, to stay up late in a neighbouring hostelry, drinking beer and shouting their opinions on the subject. Henry James, meanwhile, has long ago extinguished his light and closed his eyes – so he hopes – in sleep.

The dream, or nightmare, when it comes, is as easily remembered and as futilely repulsed, as it always is. He enters a room, a room which bears a vague resemblance to the lovely, welcoming room in De Vere Gardens where he writes his masterpieces – where, indeed, he has recently completed 'The Lesson of the Master', where the sacrifices due to high art are punitively spelt out. The room is sunny; a maid has placed spring flowers on his writing table.

Yet the bookshelves – and this is where Henry inevitably wakes and groans aloud – have been cleared completely of his books. Nothing is there of his famous library – and, worst of all, none of his own works grace the shelves.

There is one book, which stands forlornly, propped near the window at medium height. James approaches it; he knows already the title of this trespasser, this monster which has pushed out all the true and the good, all his own examples of the Real Right Thing.

He attempts to wake properly, but the dream has him in its grip again and he approaches the shelf as if he would seize the book and toss it onto the cruel stone below. *Horace Chase,* reads the title, gold lettering on a fine morocco binding. 'By Constance Fenimore Woolson'. And at last, with a dry mouth and thudding heart, he wakes.

\*     \*     \*

By the time the small figure, almost invisible in the driving rain and terrible blackness which has descended on the lake, arrives at the Hôtel de L'Ecu all the lights there are out, and the canopied restaurant, solid and majestic in its daytime guise, is folded away now, insignificant, little more than a few planks of wood jutting out over troubled water. The blank white of the façade looks disapprovingly down on Constance, as she struggles along the waterfront; and the windows, which cannot help but remind her of Henry's epithet for the windows of I Brichieri, that they are mournful when she is not there, appear sad, green-shuttered, closed like eyes in death.

Constance has no idea where she is going. The storm mounts, and seldom falls away; to plunge in the bottomless lake is tempting – but to wade out over slimy weed and sharp stones (she has tried this already) is too unbearable to contemplate. Like the hero of *Horace Chase* – which she knows, now, will be her last novel: she has told Henry about it frequently, and he has encouraged, praised, but not, as she is now convinced, with sincerity – like Jared Franklin in *Horace Chase* she needs the satisfaction of a leap from a high place, not an indecisive and soggy wading out into the deep. Jared will be rescued by the millionaire Horace – but Ruth, his spoiled wife, will kill herself, too, this time by going to the verge of a cliff and slipping over, easing her passage at first by holding onto a little sapling. It breaks and gives way, and she disappears – but for Constance, this slithering end also lacks the momentum provided by a jump from a high window. Henry must not think her death an accident; Henry, as he sits over coffee and books with his new admirers, must be aware of his Fenimore's absolute determination to end her own life.

The plot of the still unwritten *Horace Chase* takes over Constance's mind as she trudges, she knows not where or why, in thin slippers long ago reduced to pulp and swamped with water. She knows, as Ruth, the millionaire's wife had known, that she has fixed on someone totally unsuitable for her passion – not a handsome bounder, as of course the novel must provide, encouraging readers to pray for the head-strong Ruth's return to sanity and marriage with Horace – but a great man, sober and dignified, and, most important, always right. She, Constance/Fenimore, has selected – and how could she expect any other outcome than bitterness and disappointment – none other than Henry James.

Thunder, following the lightning which comes in jagged knife throws down across the lake, sounds an ominous chorus to Constance's increasingly desperate thoughts and muttered sentences. Where has she gone wrong? – was it so vulgar, really, to refer to the sainted Lizzie Boott as leaving a gentleman and a bohemian to mourn her, one the grandfather, the other the father of her child? Was it unseemly to speak of men who loved a woman, and their desolation at her going from them? Did it remind poor Henry that he is incapable of fathoming the mystery, as he has sometimes put it to her, of the nature of woman?

Poor Henry, indeed! Something in Constance resists at last, and she halts, ankle deep in lake water, feet bleeding from the sharp pebbles lurking beneath the weed. She, Constance, whose heroines, to her mentor's satisfaction, invariably choose self-immolation rather than resistance to the fate life has handed them – will at last turn from the picture of the open window, the inviting pavement below, and fight back with her own weapon, just as Henry makes his stance with his. She will save Ruth, pull her from the verge as the sapling bends and twists in her hand, give her life without the odious millionaire Horace Chase. Henry has destroyed his 'dear Fenimore' already, has he not, with his devastating and disingenuous portrait in *Harper's*, an outlet well targeted to strike at the core of Miss Woolson's huge readership. She has – and for the first time a glorious sense of freedom inhabits the breast of the modestly attired, short-statured woman standing in water under a sky lit by javelins of murderous electricity – she has simply nothing left to lose. The man to whom she has been devoted all these years had come here with the thought of marriage in his mind – Constance knows from reading his recent stories that this was the case – and he has, after destroying her career as a writer, selected an ill-turned phrase as reason not to make her his wife, either. *Basta*, as the great writer would say, when confronted with a subject no longer worth consideration.

The Villa Diodati stands above Lake Geneva; and it is in the white glare of one of the great sheets of lightning which flash from sky to hillside, that Constance sees the villa, and re-enters the story of the summer night when Shelley, his wife Mary, Lord Byron and his young mistress Claire Clairmont sat around the gardens and rooms of the house belonging to a Signor Polidori and wagered they would come up with the most frightening ghost story ever dreamed.

Mary Shelley did dream; and Constance, making her way up the hill now, through falling shale and grabbing hold of bushes as she goes, screams at the indistinct figure she sees, high by the villa's garden wall above. Frankenstein! – she sees the bolted-together monster who walked that night from Mary Shelley's mind.

Then, as another woman appears to her, and the clouds are blown away at last by wind, the moon comes out to shine on Miss Clairmont – on the young girl who grew into the old woman in Florence transformed by James into Miss Bordereau in *The Aspern Papers* – and Constance stops and stands still, in order to enjoy and understand the vision. She will go no further.

The figure by the villa wall is a guard, and his dog begins to bark. But as Constance, turning and slipping and slithering – but, unlike her heroine Ruth desperate now for life and not for death – reaches the shore of the lake and looks back one last time, she does at last understand. Henry has indeed stolen her character, to portray the sad and unappealing Miss Tina, niece of the long-dead poet's former mistress. And he has taken Claire as model for the old woman, who had been muse and 'Juliana' to his American Byron. But what is clear to Constance now, as she stumbles back the way she came, ignoring the Hôtel de L'Ecu with its slumbering genius, and making for the dark outline of the *pension*, clambering in through the window she had so carefully closed behind her in her flight – is that Claire had known the meaning of that first glorious wave of freedom when it came. She had fought and suffered –

but her life had been her own. And, by the time Miss Woolson was of an age to think and write, much later in the century, that freedom had been stolen too.

The storms have passed and Lake Geneva is flat and glassy, dutifully reflecting the Alps and a sky as clean as a newly washed china plate. There is a way in which the seeming permanence of this state of affairs affects those in the hotels and *pensions* around the lake, as well as the citizens of the town, high on the hill above the inrush of the Rhône: summer is back, everyone prospers, canopies are let down again, over cafés in the squares and cobbled walks.

The ties which bind Henry James to his 'intimate' friend seem also to be strengthened by this prolonged halcyon period. There is no mention of marriage – but nor is there any suggestion of bringing the visit to Switzerland to an end. With the patriotic sun beaming down on peaks purple and velvet – such are the descriptions coined by literary visitors – comes an assurance of promises kept and of a safe future, guarded against the depredations of darkness, violent weather and the rest. For the time being at least, both Henry and Fenimore are protected by the unexpected, almost unearthly calm.

Les Armures is an ancient hostelry atop the old town; after a brief intake of hot chocolate there, a stroll leads the tourists to the Cathedral of St Pierre, and behind that (after a steep climb) to the trees and stone platform which look out over all Geneva, the lake like a watercolour smudge in the background. The two middle-aged visitors now arriving at this point, pause for breath. They are good-humoured, but (the gentleman in particular) tire easily – and, having reserved a table at a small restaurant off the square, glance at the old clock on the great tower of the church. They have time; they are in perfect time to enjoy the prospect, before eating, and before returning, under blue skies, to their respective lodgings. There is – as if the recent storm had washed it all away – no atmosphere of expectation – whether of impending disappointment, or of bliss. Henry may have heard in a letter from his brother William that Alice, bitter and apprehensive in her carefully nurtured sickness at Leamington, has written complaining of the younger James 'flirting on the Continent with Miss Woolson', and even, in another note demonstrating her extreme displeasure, of Henry's 'gallivanting' abroad with the same dubiously regarded lady; but he evidently does not intend to rush home as a result of these charges. They are here, Miss Woolson and Mr James, in an ideal and unchanging present – without even a breath of wind to stir the robust foliage on the trees at the crest of the hill behind the cathedral.

Switzerland, so devoted to the recording of passing time, has succeeded in making it stand still.

Henry is talking of his theatrical hopes, once the friends are settled at a table (it is warm enough, yet, to sit outside on the pavement) and as he recounts his earnest desire to succeed as a playwright ('You will, Henry. Ah, you have the dramatic touch, no one has any doubt of that!' breathes Miss Woolson over her fondue) he notes that they are placed directly opposite the house which once had given shelter to

Jean-Jacques Rousseau. The narrow windows and stern façade give no hint of the great man's freeing of his spirit to write his *Confessions,* a book so astonishing that to find himself only a few yards from the walls behind which it was composed, drives Henry to a fit of absent-mindedness. Is he doing the right thing, to chase after the stage, when the written word – to be read, that is, and not performed – can alter, as Rousseau's did, the way in which the world is perceived? Is there – a worse consideration but it cannot be dodged – a single one of the works of Henry James which can bear comparison with Rousseau's *Confessions?*

Miss Woolson leans forward, to dip her little hunk of bread in the bubbling molten Gruyère, this example – and the most costly – chosen by her devoted friend, as it contains kirsch, a liqueur of which the best-selling novelist has no previous experience. The taste is sweet and strong, and scorches the throat; and, to prevent a coughing fit, Miss Woolson unbuttons her little brown tweed jacket. Her companion looks away. But, as James notes with an almost vindictive satisfaction, an image from one of Fenimore's recent letters cannot be prevented from coming to mind. He sees her hanging over the pot of fondue as she had once, so she informed him by letter, hung over the lake on her last visit to Lake Geneva. She had been Rousseau's Virginie, so she had informed him, dreaming of her love – and, in the incarnation of Miss Woolson, dreaming of Henry James.

The sun continues to shine, Fenimore, hasty and scarlet-cheeked with shame at the thoughtless revealing of such long-hidden charms as she could be said to possess, retires in order to reassemble her outfit. But by the time she is back at the table, the fondue has been removed, and replaced by a bill which her companion pays. (No – he will not for a moment entertain the idea of Fenimore putting in her Swiss francs – he insists!) And, by the mere fact of setting down his money with an air of finality, the Master ends the 'working holiday' which had worked so wonderfully well for both of them. The sun may shine – but Henry must go back, to resume his life in London and complete *The Tragic Muse*. This glorious, golden Geneva autumn must be the turning point of his – alas so far, financially unsuccessful – career.

Miss Woolson understands that the late honeymoon is over. A vision, suggesting itself pleasantly a moment before, of a resumption of the conversation, this accompanied by a slice of chocolate cake, espied already on a trolley, dark and gleaming and garnished with hazelnuts, is wrenched abruptly from the mind. 'It may appear to be summer,' Henry says in a pleasant tone, 'but it grows dark early, my dear Fenimore. One should make one's way down the hill and, as it were, out over the lake, before such a contingency should arise. Allow me to suggest one last trip by *gondole*, if I may, to your *pension*? I can deposit you there and continue to L'Ecu.'

If Miss Woolson has the impression that she is about to be deposited altogether for some time to come, she gives no indication of this. The old friends walk amicably down to the quay and there engage a boat – just as they had, so Miss Woolson cannot help reflecting with a pang, when they had first formed a bond in Venice many years ago.

Today, the lake is as smooth as the lagoon, in Miss Woolson's memory. Yet – as she sits back on the faded and, omen of the true autumnal weather about to set in, slightly damp cushions of the gondola – something comes to disturb her happy reminiscences of those Venetian days. 'This brings to mind the occasion when we went together out to Torcello,' she begins – but a picture of a woman 'taken advantage of', 'led on', comes to her and the sentence does not properly end.

'Ah yes', agrees the author. But he also sounds embarrassed and uncertain.

Constance prepares for her departure – how many there have been! – from the *pension* on Lake Leman (as Henry has told her so often she must refer to this seductive but frightening inland sea) – by herding her baskets together on one side of the bedroom and marching to the wardrobe to select the costumes she will require on her forthcoming journey to Bellosguardo. She had seen her friend flinch when she had promised to 'write, we shall have our letters to each other at least' and now wishes, as it seems she has done so often, that she had not referred to their correspondence. As a self-inflicted punishment, on passing the trunk where her most treasured possessions reside (too precious even to unpack, these consist mainly of portraits of her mother and sister and Henry's letters over the years) she kicks it viciously, and in the short time it takes to go around to the far side of the room, can already feel the bump of a bruise and the suggestion of a broken toenail.

The wardrobe door swings open, the long mirror

providing – as Constance knew it was bound to do (in this happy time out of time she had avoided the sliver of quicksilver with her reflection coming right to the edge of the glass) – confirmation of the reason for her sorrow and hurt. Even if later, in the solitude of her terrace at I Brichieri and with Florence a mute and indifferent witness to her size, Miss Woolson writes to friends that she has never felt so well, and is 'as stout as can be' – a state of affairs, it seems, the doughty novelist is glad to welcome – she experiences little jubilation now. Constance Fenimore Woolson is, to put it bluntly, a fat old sow. How could she have imagined herself as the future Mrs Henry James?

The costumes for Florence can wait. The weather still holds good; and Constance will not find herself 'deposited' at her *pension* in mid afternoon with nothing to look forward to but an early supper in the presence of a salon full of spinsters followed by a long, grey night in her room. She will walk, not along the shore as she had done on the occasion of the wild night before the golden days, but inland, seeking the comfort of the company of Claire Clairmont, another woman who had braved life alone. She will attempt to recall, as she goes, the appearance of the woman once pointed out to her in the Uffizi gallery as Miss Clairmont's niece; and the voice – yes, that was it: of Violet Paget, the novelist Vernon Lee – returns to her as she takes the road from the *pension* that goes north, in the direction of the house Signor Polidori rented in that fateful summer of 1816, the Villa Diodati. Vernon Lee (Henry is rather odd about her too, when it comes down to it: Miss Woolson might almost be tempted to think he dislikes women who write and has had to pretend not to hear him when, on being asked by an acolyte whether he believed women *could* write, he replied 'Yes very badly!') – Vernon Lee, or Miss Paget, had turned from the contemplation of a Botticelli when Constance had met her, to explain the niece. And there – Constance stops on the road, which has petered out to become little more than a track, with a scattering of summer's wild flowers on the verge – there, in her memory, in the long vastness of the gallery, walks a plain, stoutish woman in her forties. She wears a black hat and has a child with her, about thirteen years old. 'They say,' the androgynous bestseller-writer remarked to Miss Woolson (it was fortunate, Constance recollects reflecting at the time that dear Henry was not there also: he would perhaps have flinched at the sight of two women writers together) – 'they say the name of this niece of Miss Clairmont's, Hanghegyi or something of the kind, is no more than Clairmont itself in Hungarian.' 'So you mean there may be no father for the child?' Constance had replied on cue. The plots of many of the romances penned by such as Vernon Lee and herself had come back to her, as she stood trying not to gawp at the unprepossessing woman in the black hat. 'Indeed,' concurred Miss or Mr Lee. 'The daughter is illegitimate.' 'Like poor Allegra, Claire Clairmont's daughter by Lord Byron,' Constance remembers saying. She had been conscious of feeling herself trapped in the realm of the woman writer just then, even if Henry James himself would have had few scruples in taking advantage of the most lurid and romantic report of seduction and betrayal if it suited him to do so.

Paula – that had been the name of the woman so

much less – even if Constance must protest this only when quite alone – appealing than Miss Woolson. How could she, Henry's Fenimore, have taken the description of Miss Tina in *The Aspern Papers* as herself, when she can recall now, with a vision that had temporarily deserted her, each detail of the niece Paula's looks? How can she feel so offended with her dear fellow-writer, when he has, perhaps unfairly but at least it is not a portrait of *her* – painted Paula as he had doubtless heard her spoken of by Vernon Lee? 'A woman of very loose morals even when rescued by her aunt from penury, I hear': Vernon Lee's words come back to Constance now as she walks, dragging her steps, along the road. 'She became the mistress of that Shelley-spouting bore, the man who tried to get his hands on Miss Clairmont's papers. Edward Silsbee. They parted – but both are still living somewhere in Italy, I believe.'

Constance pauses at this final kick of memory, and turns to retrace her steps. She will go back to the propriety, the stifling boredom, the privacy of the *pension*. The unfortunate Paula was not the niece Henry saw when he wrote; the 'ridiculous, pathetic old woman' was not, never could be Paula. Like her aunt before her, Paula enjoyed a lusty life and cared little what the world said about it. The model for Miss Tina was herself. Henry James had changed the setting to avoid Paula identifying herself as the younger Miss Bordereau.

It does get dark early after all, in this artificial summer on the lake. Constance returns to the *pension* just as evening falls – but not without a brief, magnificent sunset to guide her in. She goes up to her room and without removing jacket, hat or scarf, sits at the bureau and takes up her pen. She begins to write.

For some time now – a year or two perhaps, since the publication in *Harper's* of 'Miss Woolson' by Henry James – anonymous (and waspish) reviews of the Master's works have been appearing in various magazines in America. For those not aficionados of the Master's *oeuvre*, the malicious short notices provide pleasure; for the disciples, astonishment prevails at the clear inner knowledge of the subject on which the unknown critic writes.

Miss Woolson begins her review of *The Aspern Papers* with an attack on one of Henry's self-confessed vulnerable areas, in this recently published tale. Jeffrey Aspern, the 'American Byron' conjured by the author, is quite simply an impossibility. At the time of Byron and Shelley in Europe, there were no great lyric poets in America, and to place Aspern then is a pure and obvious nonsense, though to set him later is also an impossibility, as the two Misses Bordereau, relics of the Romantic era, could not be the ages they are, unless these dates are adhered to. Even worse, *The Aspern Papers* demonstrates for once and for all the impotence of Mr James – a word not lightly chosen – when it comes to the understanding of the nature of womanhood. The elder Miss Bordereau, 'Juliana' to the late Jeffrey Aspern, is a mockery, a monster in a green eyeshade who has interest only in the money she can grasp from her lodger. Does the author imagine women degenerate thus in old age? His heroine, it is said, is based on none other than Claire Clairmont, friend and companion of Shelley, stepdaughter of William Godwin no less. And the 'grand-niece'? Here Miss Woolson's pen trembles, before approaching the inkpot and dipping in deep. Can the writer of this 'ridiculous and pathetic' tale not have seen how one of his own characters, Miss Tina, was the one to lead the narrator on? Hidden under this story of rapacity and greed lies a portrait not of a simple woman but of a clever one. Miss Tina had seen the game her suitor was playing all along, and the unsatisfactory ending, in which the Aspern papers are burned 'one by one', was forced on its creator by his lack of insight into the nature of the woman he had found it amusing to caricature.

Nothing had happened. There had been no drama – Fenimore can be counted on never to produce a 'scene' and she has not done so. Of course, there is no reason she should; but James, taking his last stroll in the pleasant, but now decidedly wintry gardens of the Hôtel de L'Ecu, has an uneasy sense that an undercurrent had existed, in the placid waters of their friendship. Nothing happened; yet had his dear comrade, the sole woman of his acquaintance who really can understand what he means, however obscure the text or words, been aware of giving the impression that she wanted not nothing but something after all? And if so – Henry turns briskly in the shrubbery, on seeing the valet at the window of his room (he must go in and arrange his *emballage*) – what could that something possibly be?

Thoughts of marriage, and of the violent display of rejection of Miss Woolson as his wife, this only just concealed behind a screen from the ever-interested gaze of his young male admirers on the occasion of the late cognac in the hotel, have successfully been banished from the Master's mind. If poor Fenimore had seemed – he cannot use the word 'needy', he has understood that it has crept into usage in America as a description of a person lacking affection or attention and this, surely, his much cared-for friend can hardly complain of being – if poor dear Fenimore had given, like the bat, a signal indicating need, an emotion not catered for on this supremely delightful visit to Switzerland – then Henry has, as any other man would be, found himself incapable of hearing it. The two writers had come here to ply their pens, and they have done so. Again, if the note from 'Mademoiselle Woolson', delivered to the hotel today, had seemed brusque, even strained, in its polite farewell, he had not been able to detect a true note of reproach in it. He had been relieved to learn that Fenimore's sister will come to visit at Bellosguardo – Miss Woolson's destination, as he had known. So the doughty novelist will not be left entirely to her own devices. And Henry himself, in a conversation where he had suspected he was thought to be offering too little, though Fenimore would of course never say so – had made the firm suggestion of an annual visit to Florence by himself. Is this not enough? He will stay downstairs at I Brichieri and Fenimore and he may well collaborate on a play – though Henry, now mounting the stairs and beginning his discussion of the packing with the valet, knows this is not at all likely to take place. Stay in Bellosguardo he may; but his friend surely does not need collaboration – the very word makes him shudder. He has been on the point of offering too much – and really, there is no need, as nothing happened.

The journey, in this autumn following the publication of *The Aspern Papers*, will take Henry James to Monaco, Genoa and Paris, before he arrives in London to be in De Vere Gardens by Christmas.

He finds that the theatre plays an important part in his thoughts, and when in Paris James visits the comedienne Julia Bartet on her *loge* at the Théâtre Français. The visit will prove useful for the novel in hand about the theatre, *The Tragic Muse*.

All in all, over the months following their 'idyll' on Lake Geneva, Henry thinks of Fenimore very little; though she does appear to him sometimes as a character in a story forming, before growing or dying in his mind, notably Maria Gostrey, May Bartram and poor Fanny Knocker.

# GEORGINA
## FLORENCE, 19 MARCH 1879

Aunt died today. It was about ten in the morning, Mama had gone up with a glass of water saying she'd mix in the wine herself, for Aunt had the habit of pouring in too much and saying that at eighty-one her eyesight had much to answer for. Mama said nothing, and went down to fetch Julia. She told her to go out for the doctor. But I knew already that Aunt was dead, for I'd been in her room since early, searching for the letter. By now, after all the trouble with Shelley and the papers, Claire has been keeping her famous letters in a hiding-place where even the wicked Captain Silsbee would never find them – if he had the courage to come back here, that is. I've known for a year or more that they're between the mattress and the bed, and as Aunt never got up, no one could have thought of looking for them there. I admire Aunt – but I am happy now that I can look for the letter in peace – once her body has been carried away and before Julia goes in to strip off the linen.

Then I shall be happier still. 'I will write to Claire to ask formally for your hand when you arrive at the age of consent,' Trelawny said to me on that dreadful day when Aunt's last, scorching temper flare burnt our home to a cinder, leaving only the remnants of the household when the blaze had died down: poor Mama, Julia and myself. 'You will be coming up to sixteen years of age, Georgina and we shall be married. You are to be mistress of my house in Kensington,' Trelawny said.

So I wait, in the little dining-room that is freezing cold on this March day, even if pear and quince trees in blossom can be seen in the della Robbias' garden through the window. It's as if the death of that last spark from those days my beloved Edward lived and still in his heart enjoys (these are words about himself the great adventurer taught me, before he left) – it's as if Aunt has brought this frost to Florence by deciding to go at long last to her grave. 'I have seen enough, Georgina, and I die in penury,' Aunt said. She had just enough strength in her, at daybreak this morning, to play her old dramatic role; and when she winked at me then I knew she understood very well what I had come up to look for.

The two remaining old men – Silsbee having run from Mama's clutches some time ago – were thrown out of our house on the same day, the day the nun came and said she was Allegra. Well, it was a trick played by my fiancé Edward Trelawny – who will take me to London to a fine neighbourhood, and make me his wife and hostess to the great who come to hear his memories. It was a trick that was perhaps a little cruel, but Edward said it was done for Claire's good. She had to learn that the bee in her bonnet, as Edward put it, was to be got rid of at all costs. 'This is why I came all the way to Italy at my great age,' Trelawny said, 'to persuade my old friend that she would not care for a female monster following her about, an old woman who bore no resemblance to Claire's darling little Allegra.' I knew this wasn't the sole reason for Edward's visit: he was as much up in Aunt's room as Mr Silsbee, demanding recollections of Byron or Shelley for his records – but he certainly found a novel way of frightening Aunt out of her obsession that her daughter is still alive. 'Imagine, my dear Claire,' all the house could hear Trelawny spouting to Aunt in the days before he took me along to the convent at Bagnocavallo and engaged the wretched nun to play her part in his little trick at Via Romana. 'Can you conceive a greater horror than an old man or woman you had never seen for fifty-five years, claiming you as Mother?' 'Oh leave me in peace, Edward,' Aunt would say – when she wasn't pretending to be deaf and so refusing to hear a word Trelawny said to her.

The nun posing as Allegra came as the last straw and Mama was told to see off Edward Trelawny, Claire's most devoted lifelong admirer, as well as the indefatigable blackmailer, Luigi Gatteschi. The Italian had come back to 43 Via Romana just as Trelawny was burning the love letter Mary Shelley had written to him all those years ago in Paris, in the grate. It was a hot summer day, and Signor Gatteschi, with his fat stomach that Julia says shows he has no one to look after him, arrived just too late to rescue the letter from the flames. He went down on his hands and knees as if he could restore Mary Shelley's words of passion. But not even a corner of the letter or its envelope remained. As this scene took place just after the entrance of the nun – and Trelawny ran up the stairs two at a time to introduce Claire to her 'daughter' who followed him, there was no time either to condemn or feel pity for the rogue. He had lost his last chance of extorting money from Claire Clairmont, it was true – but then, as I could have told Luigi all along, Aunt had none anyway.

When they came down together – Claire, who so seldom left her room, Trelawny and the veiled figure who was, I suppose, sent back to the convent and her Mother Superior once Mama had shown her the door – it was as if a whole flock of pigeons had fallen down the stairwell. Aunt was exploding with rage; the nun, all in black and by now very agitated, was giving little coos and cries which showed she understood nothing of the scenario she found herself in; and Trelawny was laughing one of those great laughs Julia says will surely carry him off in an apoplexy one day. I stood in the hall, helpless, and I must have seemed a child to Aunt again, because she stopped midway down the last flight and pointed her finger at me. 'This is the daughter I have chosen to adopt,' she said then, in a very loud voice, so Luigi crept from his contemplation of the sitting-room grate to catch a glimpse of the woman who had foiled his plan to expose and shame – or be paid by – her sister Mary all that time ago. 'Now you must go, Edward' – and, on seeing Gatteschi, successfully concealed from her up to then – 'Out with you, sir! Kindly leave my house!'

So it was, as I say, that we found our ménage reduced to what it had been before. And now it is reduced further, for Aunt has gone and when I have found the letter in her room which asks for my hand from Edward Trelawny, I shall write down his address in London and go there to marry him whether Mama says I may or not.

Now I am told once more that I may not go upstairs. There has always been a good reason given – and early on I came to understand that I should not go there in case I overheard Aunt's conversations with Silsbee; for they were indelicate in the extreme, so Julia and the friends who came to visit her in the kitchen said. Aunt was an atheist, at the time I was a small child, for one thing – and the meaning of that word took a long time to discover – but then she converted to the Catholic faith, so for quite a time now there was surely no danger in my going up to visit her. Only when I was of use to Mama and Silsbee, and was asked to fetch – or in rare circumstances return – a letter or manuscript, was I encouraged to visit the room of the woman all Florence liked to gossip about.

Now Aunt is dead I can see no reason for Mama's ban. Is it because no one knows yet whether Aunt died a pagan or a Christian? 'Father Weld is of a famous English family,' my mother said last New Year's Day, as if the eminence of the visiting priest's origins would surely impress the old woman and make her decide to see him. But the ban was on Father Weld on that occasion, and Aunt called for me instead. Had she originally converted, as she mischievously informed Mr Silsbee – as he told all of us later while sipping the American whisky he liked to bring into the house and measure out for no one but himself – had Aunt become a papist in order to go as a *pensionnaire* all those years ago to the convent at Bagnocavallo and be with her little daughter Allegra? When their plan failed, she suffered a lapse of faith and only recently had asked Father Weld to take her into the Church. Mama had been astonished and Julia very pleased. But, just three months before deciding to give up the last gasps of her life, Claire had refused to see Father Weld and he had gone away with a flea in his ear, just like the other old men she'd thrown out of her home. 'It would have been a fine thing if Aunt had been exorcised,' Mama said in a grim tone on the occasion of Father Weld's last – and unsuccessful – visit.

In an hour or so, according to Julia, the undertakers will come for Aunt and she will leave 43 Via Romana feet first, as she has often joked she looked forward to doing. 'Then the bailiffs will find it hard to hand a writ to a pair of feet,' she would say, while Mama's eyes roamed uncomfortably over the cupboard, trying – so I surmised – to figure out where the will was kept, and how much Shelley, after all the fuss and bother about the past, would eventually be worth. 'As for you, Paula dear, you will have to go back to work as a governess or a companion to an old lady or something of the sort,' Aunt would say, and her eyes would light up with spite. Mama was angry a long time afterwards: there must surely be something left to her in the will, she'd complain to us downstairs, after all these years of labour and what she refers to as selfless devotion? 'Don't count on it,' Aunt would say when my mother was smoothing her bed and trying to restore order in the room, and she'd go off into one of her coughing, wheezing fits. For Aunt used to guess each time my mother got the pensive look that meant she was thinking about money.

Now, however, I have little time left, and must go up there even if Mama tries to stop me and pulls me by the hair. So I scream and make a fuss like the eight-year-old she pretends I am. It is Mama, I know, who is jealous of the attentions paid me by Mr Trelawny; Mama who misses Edward Silsbee, whom she would call an angel on the days he spoke of nothing but poetry and love, and a devil when he refused her her heart's desire, namely marriage and a secure future (though even a child like myself could see that there was no such thing as a settled life with the old sea-captain). So Mama will do all she can to destroy Trelawny's proposal of marriage to her daughter – her 'little Georgina' who must remain confined at Via Romana and will never be permitted to find a new life. When the letter is found, my wicked, lying Mama will scrumple it in a ball and throw it into the fire in Aunt's room, this kept in by Julia, who puts juniper branches on the embers to freshen the air there. Mama will, quite simply, do all she can in the world to prevent her own daughter from going to London and becoming a great hostess in Kensington.

I wait my time – for Mama, as I have heard her say to Julia, will go out shortly to find fresh flowers for Aunt's grave and to talk to the priest about the funeral service, which is to be as unostentatious and inexpensive as possible. I wait, reading the Bible which my mother pressed into my hands last night, as Aunt was visibly preparing herself for the next world, a place Shelley said had provided no evidence as proof of its existence. I hear the usual scuffle in the hall as Mama and Julia argue – this time, it is true, in whispers – as to the nature of the foodstuffs required for the household today. Then the door closes, again more quietly than usual, and Mama has gone.

I am surprised to find myself so calm and collected when I finally do arrive in Aunt's room, unheard and unmolested by Julia or by any of the other black-clad women of her family, who seem to have appeared out of thin air as if summoned by a tolling bell only they can hear. I pause a moment on the threshold, expecting the sadness I had been warned of, by Mama, who is all piety now, and greedy also for the reading of the will later. 'I feel compunction for the child,' Mama announced to the doctor as he left – in a hurry as always – we are poor here and he had no wish to accept Julia's offer of a chipped cup containing watered-down coffee. 'Georgina was her aunt's favourite, you know.' But the doctor had no wish to know. And I see now, as I look anxiously over at the bed where the body lies, that Aunt is not able any longer to know me or anything about me, either.

Her eyes – those large eyes which used to remain half-open, seeing or not-seeing the Shelley-seekers as they tiptoed around her bed – are closed. But I cannot indulge myself in dreaming of the sights those eyes saw, Shelley plain or otherwise. I have to find the letter from Trelawny, promising Aunt that he wishes to marry me and to keep me safe, far from his other wives, as Mama sardonically dismissed his proposal to me, at the time. 'Join the gypsies and the daughters of Greek thieves and bandits if you will, Georgina. But I shall do all in my power to prevent you from seeing Edward Trelawny again.'

It does not take long to move Aunt, frail as the wasted corpse of a bird, on the bed where she has lain all day in recent months. It appeared, on the occasions I would steal upstairs to see her, that she guarded the press, so often and trustingly opened for Silsbee or for a handsome young journalist, such as William Graham, with her body and her unwavering gaze. And the shadow of the shutter at the window, falling on Aunt's face at those times made a dark band across those famous eyes – as if she hid herself, in turn, from the scrutiny of the dead. I had wished sometimes to remove this illusion of a green eyeshade which seemed to obscure her true expression from me, but I had not dared. Now, there is no question of such storytelling or daydreaming in her presence. For I alone know where Aunt's treasure lies – and it's not in her wardrobe at all. I have to lift and move the white legs, slender as the spills used by Mama or Julia to light the fire that now fades in her grate. I have to slide my hands beneath the uneven mattress and feel for the letters. And at last I find paper, yielding and brittle as Aunt's aged skin, and pull out the letters, and then find I must crawl to a further reef where manuscript books, sharp-edged, lurk above the foundation of the bed.

It is not there. I cannot believe my darling Edward neglected to write to Claire on the all-important subject of his own future and of mine – and I glide through the years of his protestations to her as if this past love could throw some light on what I should await from the great man (for this I know him to be). He asks Claire many times over the past half century to marry him (she writes back and says No!) and once to come to England to be 'housekeeper to my houseless self'. He offers Aunt his letters from Shelley (the poet's heart he donates to Mary). But – as I realise slowly – Claire and Trelawny are too alike to live together. She spins her stories; and he his. If they married, would he persuade her, as he tries to do in his letters, to write her memoir of Shelley? 'I shall join Shelley's letters with a clear, plain narrative,' she writes to him, but she never did so: would Trelawny as a husband have made her take up her pen? It seems more likely that her friend would have considered himself proprietor of all she wrote, and would have made use of it for his *Recollections*.

I take the letters, the records of Aunt's love of Shelley and her hatred of Byron as she informs Trelawny of her trials at Geneva copying out *Childe Harold* while 'Albé' boasts of a future seduction of his Allegrina and hints at an incestuous union with his sister – I scoop up the letters and the manu-scripts and return them to their tin box in the press. I want no more of those times, I must live now. And as I pull from the recesses of the cupboard the grey cobweb that is the shawl Claire was given more than half a century ago by Shelley, my mother comes up the stairs and enters the room and sees me standing here. 'Whatever are you doing with that filthy rag?' she says in a sharp tone. Then I see the lawyer – he has been here before, summoned by Aunt when she decided to make her will – as he reaches the landing outside and pauses a moment, unsure whether he should come in. Behind him, late as Julia had prophesied they would be, pant the undertaker's men. 'Let us arrange all this as quietly as possible,' Mama says; and I see her, for the first time, as youthful, handsome and determined, no longer the woman in the black hat that other girls of my age would laugh at when we went on an expedition to the Pitti or the Uffizi, pretending as we walked past the pictures that we had an interest in Art. Aunt's death has already altered my mother, smoothed her wrinkles and cleared the frown from between her eyes. 'Georgina – put that rag in the fire,' Mama goes on. But it takes Julia, arriving last in the suddenly crowded room, to spell out Aunt's wishes. Aunt desired to be buried with the shawl Shelley had given her, Julia said – and I could see, in my mother's eyes as she heard this, a new look of impatience and scorn. I understood then that all sentiment had vanished from Mama's life completely, and that she intended in future to do as she pleased.

This change in the character and resolution of Paula Hanghegyi was not, however, known to all who came to call on us in the time following that day at no. 43 Via Romana.

# GEORGINA
## FLORENCE, JULY 1879

It is hot again, making me think of poor Aunt, buried now at Antello, a good three miles south-east of Florence, so Mama goes seldom to visit the grave, saying she has to save money while the fight for the spoils goes on. And a fight it is, with the heat leading me to dream of Fiesole, where Aunt used to go in summer if she could afford it. 'Everything will work out in the end,' Mama says, still her new self and confident we shall all live like kings on the proceeds of Shelley. 'It's a question of waiting for Mr Newman to come to his senses and pay up. He may be an agent, but he should buy the papers directly for the sum we are expecting. Then he may resell. We would be better off then than sitting around like this and having to endure all the chopping and changing.'

I can't help but agree with this. Every day brings a new twist and turn in the negotiations. Mr Buxton Forman will come on a Tuesday, and Mr Newman a day later. Then the executor, Signor Cini, comes just when it is least convenient, on a sultry evening when Julia and I have our feet in bowls of cold water in the kitchen and Mama is curling her hair. 'Your aunt has bequeathed me Shelley's inkstand,' says Cini in his mournful voice that makes me want to burst out laughing. 'But the pen will not go in it, Signorina Georgina. There must be some mistake – this cannot be the inkstand of the most exalted poet who ever lived amongst men.' These visits and conversations make me homesick for Aunt, if such an expression makes sense: 'Oh, Shelley knew the pen only went in one side,' I hear her pleasant, amused voice with a tinge of malicious humour in it, too. Somehow, when I try to explain the peculiarities of Mr Cini's bequest to him, it doesn't sound so convincing.

The truth of the matter is that we are getting nowhere with the sale of the papers. Mr Buxton Forman and Mr Newman go off in a huddle together when they happen to coincide – and sometimes voices are raised. But the letters from Shelley to Claire, and the letters from Mary to Claire and the letters from Claire to Godwin and all the rest, including the manuscript notebooks that were so important to Aunt, just don't seem to have any price that anyone can agree on.

It was only about a week or so after Aunt died that there was a knock on the door in Via Romana. I happened to be on the middle landing, looking down for no good reason at the Boboli Gardens below and wishing the trees would get green quickly, and my grieving for Aunt would lessen with their putting on of leaves, when I saw what appeared to be a familiar head on the doorstep below. The knocking started up again. It must have been about five in the afternoon, when Julia often slips out to the church – or that, at least, is where she says she goes in the early evenings. A few days ago I found a page torn out of one of the Shelley notebooks at the bottom of her basket and confronted her with it. But she started to cry, and Mama was summoned: the page, so it was said, had dropped from a manuscript Mr Newman had returned to us and Julia had just been to market, so she had saved the page, totally illegible to her, and thought no more of it. But I do wonder now whether Shelley will last much longer all in one piece, and last night I dreamt that fragments and quartos and sonnets all fluttered down to the Piazza Signoria and then went in a great funnel of wind into the Duomo, where they became pigeons. Doesn't everyone want a piece of this treasure, so prized by scholars and poetry-lovers that no accurate value can be placed on it? As if to answer that question, I had found Mr Newman here the day before, locking the press by Aunt's now stripped and desolate-looking bed with a new padlock. 'There's been poking about here again,' Mr Newman said when I asked him the reason for this added security. But what he meant I didn't have the sense to guess.

Nor was it obvious, when I looked down at the great head with its mane of white hair and the gargantuan shoulders which were all that was visible of the figure on the doorstep, that this visitor was the man referred to as wishing to 'poke about' by Mr Newman and therefore undesirable. In fact, I felt a flutter of excitement at the man I thought I *did* recognise standing there: none other than Edward Trelawny. I may have, like Mama, changed – as indeed I trust I have – since the days of my foolish and unrealistic desire to marry the man whose heart had been given all those years ago to Claire Clairmont – but to find him there in the flesh on our own doorstep was a different matter. I felt mired down, to be frank, in the impasse created by the sale or non-sale of the letters. Would Mama have money to rent a *piano nobile* of a palazzo in Rome, as she had promised me she would do? Would my education now proceed, as Aunt had wished? Was I to have a Ball? Who would teach me to dance?

I flew down to open the door, but Julia must have just come in, and she stood there very grim-faced, holding the door just an inch or so ajar. 'No,' I heard Julia say. 'La Signora Paula? *Non e qui.*'

That was when, pushing past Julia and opening the door, I realised my mistake. For the huge, bluff, silver-bearded man who stood there was not Edward Trelawny, but Captain Silsbee; and as he came past me I half fell against the wall at the impact of his familiar, loathsome smell: tobacco, unwashed socks and an odour that was solely his, the smell of greed and eagerness.

I am lying in bed. I cannot stay up any longer, confined to the gloomy, stifling little dining-room while Mama and Silsbee talk next door in the *salone*. I heard Mr Newman say only yesterday that Mama had confided to him that she 'is not afraid of Silsbee' – and therefore, Newman confided to Mr Buxton Forman (both men are in and out here every day, driving Julia insane with the dust and chaos they bring about) that he is sure that she *is* frightened of him, and that the grizzled sea-captain has a hold on poor Mama. But I cannot think why Mama should have had anything to fear from Silsbee in the first place. Unless . . . but the thought is too repulsive to be worth consideration . . . unless Silsbee's hold over Mama is to do with those times in the little room off the kitchen where they would go together in the hope that no one would discover their lovemaking. Always after a manuscript book had been secured; and I the one who had been sent to get it! If Mama, for all her bad behaviour in those days, is to be punished by a fear of Edward Silsbee, then I shall come to her rescue. For the first time, I believe, in all my life, I wish to protect my mother as once I had wished to help and care for Aunt.

I go to the door of the *salone* but there is no need to stoop to the keyhole. Silsbee's voice has as much of a trumpet-twang as ever, and is as sincere, to my ears at least, as the voice of a mountebank at a fair advertising his fake medicines and elixirs. That he is proposing marriage to my mother is also evident; and I have to clasp my hands together so the nails bite deep into the flesh, rather than throw open the door and walk in.

'I have no doubt you consider that to propose to me at this time is no less than an heroic act,' Mama says, quiet but still perfectly audible. 'But the answer, I regret to inform you, Captain Silsbee, can only come as a disappointment.'

A silence follows: I imagine Silsbee's great, protuberant eyes fixed in bafflement on the woman who had so brief a time ago been willing to obey and acquiesce in all he did. 'My dear Mrs Hanghegyi,' the New

England voice resumes, but with more passion this time, and even a dash of hesitancy thrown in. 'It was not in my power to suggest an arrangement involving the household before. There was the education of Georgina to consider, was there not? Now, to judge by her much improved appearance, she is ready to go out in the world. We shall be alone together, Paula.'

'You shall have neither myself nor the Shelley papers,' Mama says; and now I do bend, eye to the keyhole, and see to my horror that Aunt's tin box stands on the table in the middle of the room. Had Newman locked the press in Aunt's room when it was already emptied? Can she? – for I see her go to the fireplace, where dear Edward burned Mary Shelley's passionate letter to the blackmailer Gatteschi – and I see her take a lit candle which stands on the mantel there and carry it over to the box – can Mama mean to *burn* the Shelley papers, one by one?

'Please, Paula.' Silsbee moves ponderously towards her. 'Please, my dear, consider my proposal seriously. As your husband I will care for you and young Georgina.'

I have never been so proud of Paula Hanghegyi as I find myself today. For, after opening the padlock on the tin box, Mama pulled out a letter and held it by the candle flame, so near that scorch marks showed on the ancient paper, thin and stained as if it had been dropped in the sea.

'Captain Silsbee,' she said in a voice I wished Aunt could have heard just once from her niece, for there was no petulance in it, only dignity. 'I have informed you already that you must pay for the papers if you wish to acquire them –'

'But I have no money!' Silsbee's terror cracks the trumpet sound and I have to put my hand to my mouth to stop myself from laughing out loud. 'Will you take a promissory note, Paula?' the foolish old man went on to say.

Poor Silsbee! He is gone, with his promissory notes intact – for Mama, confirming my suspicion that she had a mind to burn the papers if he did not leave the house instantly, has rid us of this false suitor for ever. When he had gone, and I came out of my hiding-place under the stairs, and once the front door was closed behind him, we fell into each other's arms.

All of which, you might say, makes a beautiful story; but another month has passed and we have the company of Mr Newman and Mr Buxton Forman every day, so all we talk and breathe is selling Shelley.

# HENRY
## VENICE, JANUARY 1894

What is very evident is that she was at the time absolutely out of her mind with fever and illness (had influenza); but it's far the more miserably to be gathered that this had supervened on a condition of chronic and absorbing melancholy which was not the consequence of anything in her situation (though it was perhaps sharpened by loneliness) but which those who knew her well (not merely encountering her socially) were painfully familiar with and always apprehensive, or at least anxious about.

*Letter from Henry James to Elizabeth Gaskell Norton*
*on 'Miss Woolson's tragic death'.*
(Unpublished Houghton MS).

Constance Fenimore Woolson's body was found on the pavement below the window in the Casa Semitecolo on the Grand Canal in Venice, from which she had jumped at midnight on 24 January. She had spent the previous weeks alone in Venice, moving from lodgings to furnished apartments – and had been seeking an unfurnished apartment to settle in. I Brichieri in Florence had been given up; and Venice, where Henry's 'Fenimore' had been happy twelve years before, was perhaps to have provided her – and her Pomeranian dog Othello – with a permanent home.

No one can know to what extent the winter gloom of the city may have contributed to Constance's anguish and despair; any more than it is possible to gauge the seriousness of the 'influenza' which James blamed for her finally going 'out of her mind' and leaping from the window of Casa Semitecolo. What is certain is that guilt and panic, once the suggestion appeared in the press that Miss Woolson had taken her own life purposely, rather than succumbing to the hallucinations of a fever, descended on James and made it impossible for him to travel out there to attend the funeral. He could not be held responsible, of course, for the death of his 'extremely intimate' friend; but he felt a horror all the same, that his promise of an annual visit to her in Florence had not been enough to assuage the pangs of solitude she suffered, these aggravated by an increasing deafness. He had not given his Fenimore the attention she craved – nor, as he knew, but did not confide to those who offered their condolences, the commitment and love she had expected and (silently) demanded of him. After the death of his sister Alice, Miss Woolson had looked to him more; and he had given neither more nor less than before. Now, it was too late.

It is February and the sun appears in the Piazza for no more than a couple of hours in the middle of the day, bringing a flush to the Doges' Palace and shining down with a chilly splendour on the *gondole* waiting for a customer to emerge from sparse crowds. Children run in and out of Florian's, and the pigeons of the Piazza, winter-hungry, gather where scraps of food are thrown, near boats bobbing by their stakes at the side of the lagoon. When a group of tourists, rising and falling on the small bridges of the Schiavoni, burst out chattering and laughing, the birds rise in what sounds like a rustle of ball-dresses, of the taffetas and silks worn in the last decade, the late 1880s when Henry James visited the Palazzo Barbaro and redrafted *The Aspern Papers* in the library there.

Now, nearly seven years later, Mrs Gardner has taken over the Palazzo and Henry, comforted by the presence of another familiar figure, the gondolier Tito, looks benignly back at the Barbaro as Tito conveys him out past the Salute to the middle of the lagoon. There had been an invitation to stay with the inimitable Isabella, descendant, as she likes to claim, of Stuart kings, at the Barbaro – but Henry has not arranged to revisit the place where the Misses Bordereau, first conceived in Florence while James was staying under Miss Woolson's roof, received confirmation of their home. After a visit from the author, the dim, expatriate ladies were placed in a suitably unfashionable district, in Rio Marin. James comes to Venice, anyway, for a very different reason than that of creating or refining a work of fiction drafted while lying – in a scorching scirocco as he recalls – under a pink mosquito net in the great library of Palazzo Barbaro. He comes to assist the Benedicts, relatives of the late Constance Fenimore Woolson, Americans who would be at a loss as to how to sort out their cousin's affairs without a man of the world to inform them: he is, as he has made plain to several worried correspondents, dedicating at least two weeks to work he has never before undertaken, that of sifting and clearing, retaining and throwing away. The panic and guilt of the preceding month have turned to action. And now, some would say fortunately, February is cold, even for this city accustomed to shiver in winter beneath the Austrian Alps. A fire will be needed every day, in the rooms in Casa Semitecolo where Fenimore worked, wrote and hoarded her possessions in baskets, hampers, valises, baskets and trunks. It is possible to burn some, at least, of her papers and letters, even if the Benedicts, understandably but annoyingly, like to keep hold of pretty well everything.

Today it is close on a fortnight since the Semitecolo, kept sealed until the arrival of the Benedicts and Henry James, was opened up for cleaning and inspection. James's acquaintance in Venice are at first compassionate, but then become intrigued, at the thorough manner in which the great man performs his task of selection and disposal. He has been seen covered in dust – or ash – as he hurries to the Casa Biondetti, where an apartment recently leased by Fenimore is his temporary home while assisting his old friend's relatives in their arduous efforts. His friends admire Henry – but, being either Venetian or American-Venetian, they begin to whisper as to the reason for the Master's extreme diligence in overseeing the final destination of Miss Woolson's effects. Did the famous author perhaps know of something which could cause him anxiety, in the Semitecolo? Not so much, it was put forward, something he needed to hide, as a thing – or letter – he did not wish anyone to find?

This is the last day of the work to be accomplished at

the palazzo where Fenimore ended her life; and James sits back with some satisfaction in the gondola as Tito, with long, deep strokes, takes him and his cargo out into the widest part of the lagoon. There had been something of a row – an altercation would perhaps be the better term – with the Benedicts before departure: they had tried to insist on taking Fenimore's last packet of papers and several of her dresses back with them to America, and James had pointed out that so many boxes had gone there already that expense and delay could only ensue if they insisted. He, Henry James and dear friend of the late Fenimore, would do what he considered to be best.

The dresses refuse to go down, at first. Like black balloons – as Henry, an old man at the end of his life, will confide to a child in Venice, daughter of resident Americans, who catches him giggling at the memory – like black pods the sleeves of Miss Woolson's black dresses fill with the water of the lagoon and come up again and again. The skirts swell, black in black water. At last, they sink, to lie undisturbed along with Fenimore and Henry's letters – which sank and disappeared so easily.

# POSTSCRIPT

It is Constance Fenimore Woolson – and not Claire
Constantia Jane Clairmont – who lies near Shelley in
the Protestant cemetery in Rome. Violets bloom all
year round there, and the cypresses placed by Trelawny
(who lies there too: he had tried to persuade Mary
Shelley to share his narrow bed, but has ended up
alone) still stand – or their descendants do, at least.

Claire Clairmont has fared less well. Her grave at
Antello, a burial site chosen for one of the Catholic
faith, as she had reluctantly become, has been removed
to make way for urban development. She lies beneath
a paving stone marking only the dates of her birth
and death.

The Shelley Papers: An inventory of papers sold to
Forman through Newman for £150 includes 23 letters
from Shelley to Claire Clairmont, 23 letters from
Shelley to Godwin, 11 letters from Percy Florence
Shelley, a lock of Shelley's hair and a small quantity
of Shelley's ashes. These relics are accessible to readers
of the manuscript collection in the British Library.

Henry James, while disposing of all those letters concerning his friendship with Constance Woolson which

he considered it necessary to destroy, nevertheless did in the end keep something of outstanding value from the Casa Semitecolo: this was the germ for one of his most famous and successful stories, 'The Beast in the Jungle', and was taken from an outline in a notebook of Fenimore's: 'To imagine a man spending his life looking for and waiting for his "splendid moment". "Is this my moment?" "Will this state of things bring it to me?" But the moment never comes. When he is old and infirm it comes to a neighbour who has never thought of it or cared for it.'